CLAIMING SARAH

DANIELS DUET
BOOK ONE

MAE K. KNIGHT

ALSO BY MAE K. KNIGHT

LASHER BROTHERS DUET

Surviving Zaine

Escaping Xavier

DANIELS DUET

Claiming Sarah

Meating Dalton

SINS OF THE LASHER FAMILY

Breaking Elizabeth

Training Xander

TABOO TALES

Daddy's Girl

Call Me Weirdo

Tempting Uncle Maddox

Resisting My Brother

Still Daddy's Girl

Claimed By My Sister

Catch Me, Freak

TRIGGER WARNINGS

This book contains sensitive material relating to:
Reverse age gap
Kidnapping
Blood/gore/violence/mutilation
Cheating (Not MCs)
Child neglect/abandonment/abuse
Discussion of fertility issues
Pregnancy
Drugging
Anxiety (and medication for it)
Night terrors/PTSD
Dub-con/non-con
Sexual assault (off-page, not FMC)
Somnophilia
Stalking
Murder
Corpse dismemberment
Mental health disorders/hallucina-
tions/compulsions/Delusions
Self-harm
House Fire

Death by snake
Death by bees
Torture
Grief — Parental death
Cannibalism
Entomophagy

PLAYLIST

Crazy — Natalie Jane
The Fire — Bishop Briggs
Big White Room — Jess
Hold My Hand — Lady Gaga
Dark Side — Bishop Briggs
How Do I Say Goodbye — Dean Lewis
Chokehold — Austin Giorgio
KNIVES — Neoni, Savage Ga$p
On your knees — Ex Habit
Put It On Me — Matt Maeson
Be Your Love — Bishop Briggs
Iris — The Goo Goo Dolls
See You Again (ft. Charlie Puth) — Wiz Khalifa

DEDICATION

For anyone looking for an escape from their mind, from the dark place. You're not alone.

CONTENTS

1
BUZZING

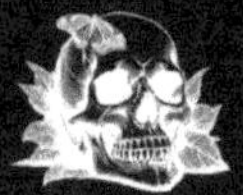

ZAIDEN

Buzzing, nearly loud enough to drown out screams, bounce off the hollow walls. Dr. Moore struggles against his restraints, to no avail. Leather bites into his wrists, skin scraped raw from his frantic movements. Dried blood stains the black bands of the handcuffs. Cocking my head, I briefly consider investing in metal cuffs over leather. Maybe they wouldn't agitate the skin as much.

"It doesn't matter. He knows."

"Break him. Crack him open."

"I want to see his insides."

"You are so fucked. He knows nothing. You'll be alone forever."

Darkness descends as I close my eyes on the voices, phantom fingers trailing down my neck. But I know there's no one here. Daniels' Manor always held ghosts, but not of the supernatural variety.

It's all in your head, Zaiden, I remind myself, shaking my head. The buzzing doesn't let up. The agitated nest of bees continues swarming against their glass enclosure in my grip. My gloved hands clutch the glass jar tighter. Setting the jug down carefully on a tray near the examination table Dr. Moore stretches out on, I turn my curious eyes on the clinician.

"P-p-please. Don't do this. I told you everything I know about Dr. Bell. I don't know anything else!" His passionate wail provides a chorus to the buzzing and whispers in my head.

"Release them. Let them fly free."

"They want to be free, Zaiden."

"You won't find your brothers if you don't free them."

Shadows race across the walls of the room, taking the shape of an oversized bee, mandibles opening and closing, snapping at the shadow of Dr. Moore's head. It turns red eyes on me, malice oozing from its shadowy body. Nodding, I run quick hands over myself, ensuring my gear is in place.

"Please! Somebody help me!" Dr. Moore continues his screams for help.

"Please, somebody help me," I whimper, curling into a fetal position on the thin cot beneath me. A threadbare blanket does nothing to keep the chill out. Tremors crawl over me, vibrating the bed. My mouth opens, screams and gnarled hands crawling out, ripping me open.

"No," I whisper at no one, curling my fingers into fists. I am free. Before I could change my mind, quick as a breeze, I snatch the lid off the bee enclosure, stepping back, letting the swarm fly free.

Dr. Moore's struggles intensify, and so do his screams. It reminds me of my mother, screaming at open doorways, cradling me to her chest. Little Brother would watch us with wary eyes, huddled in a separate corner. The past clutches at me, threatening to suction me into the abyss, where the jagged lines of reality blur, bleeding into a distorted puddle.

Puddle. Puddle. My head jerks. I need to get away from Dr Moore and the bees. Stiff legs carry me away, boots pounding into the tiled flooring. The rusted green door creaks open, the sound competing with Dr. Moore's high-pitched screams.

I could glance back, but I already know what I'd find. The poor doctor has a lethal bee allergy. If the numerous stings don't cause his throat to swell to the point of asphyxiation, then the venom should kill him. Once his flesh is nice and swollen, I'll peel it open to harvest the organs. They possess an exorbitant amount of nutritional value.

The door slams shut behind me, echoing through the barren walls of Daniels' Manor.

SARAH

"Lauren, you are ruining your life!" I snap at my stubborn child. My fingers tighten on the phone clutched in my hands, eyes squeezed shut, praying for patience. Patience. If my sister, Natalia, overheard me asking for patience, she'd laugh. Phantom aches twinge through my fingers. I lost count of how many raps on the knuckles I received as a child for rushing through my schoolwork, mind moving faster than my body.

"Mom, what do you expect me to do? Go back to work and pretend nothing ever happened? This can be a fresh start for me. Please, I'm only asking for you to not speak to the police, to not make things worse. However, I am not asking for your permission." Lauren's tone hardens over the phone, a neon sign waving at me, signaling her heels have dug in, and resistance is futile.

I let out a curse, ignoring the snicker on the other line from my single-minded child. But she's not a child anymore, is she? Exhaustion rests on my back, amplifying the force of gravity.

Voices whisper back and forth in the small space of the break room in Mercy Hospital. A news reporter drones on about the weather, the muted sound from the television speakers never reaching me, too lost in wondering where I went wrong with Lauren.

"I do not agree with this." My voice wavers slightly, but I straighten my back, forcing steel into my tone, pulling on years of dealing with unruly patients and a temperamental child, masking my emotions.

"I will make up my own mind on what I'll do should I cross that bridge. I won't make any promises." I rub a hand over weary eyes, sliding the skin of my eyelids to scrape across the round surface of my eyeballs. It does nothing to stall the headache aiming for me from the terse conversation with Lauren.

"Just be safe. Call me when you're somewhere safe," I plead in a soft voice, heart aching, yearning to stretch across the distance separating us and pull her into my arms.

"I will, Mom. I promise. I love you," Lauren says, a small crack entering her voice. Emotions clog my throat but I force myself to croak the words back, "I love you, too." Trembling fingers end the call before I begin sobbing at my job.

Rising from my chair, I pick up the uneaten salad that was my lunch before Lauren called with news she was leaving for Mexico with a known killer. I walk to the trash, tossing the unappealing spread of lettuce and my expectations for Lauren into the can. A mother can only do so much. I ignore the voice whispering in my head, *but she's not your biological child, is she?*

I shove the dark voice away, walking out of the breakroom and giving my coworkers a tight smile. Natalia and Lauren share a similar skin color and I love them as if they're my flesh and blood. Only failed IVFs encourage the insidious whispers. An inability to conceive a child on my own whittled away at the hope of providing Lauren with a sibling.

Xavier Lasher has taken my only child from me, maybe the only child I'll ever have as menopause hurtles toward me in my mid-forties. Walking to the nurses' station, I note the irony of me delivering children for a living but appearing unable to carry one of my own.

"Has anyone seen Dr. Moore?" I ask no one in particular, approaching a vacant chair in front of a desktop.

"Nope," Natasha calls, lips popping on the p, drawing my eye to her heavy makeup. I bite my tongue, refusing to remind her yet again of hospital policy concerning makeup and false nails. Each jab of her two-inch long nails into the keyboard stabs into my brain, irritating the oncoming headache.

Where the fuck is Dr. Moore? I wonder, rubbing at my temples. The end of the shift can't come soon enough.

2
RAVEN

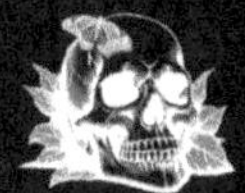

ZAIDEN

She's pretty.

"Take her."

"Break her."

The whispers grow in volume, but staring down at Dr. Bell's sleeping form, their hold loosens, skirting the edges of my fractured mind. Dark lashes rest on high cheekbones. Alabaster skin catches stray rays of moonlight slipping through the cracks of the curtains in her bedroom. I lean closer, inhaling.

Faint traces of vanilla float in the air, sliding through the holes of my nostrils and burrowing into my brain. My tongue swipes across my lips for a taste. I jerk back at the unexpected reaction. A taste of what? I tilt my head down at the sleeping beauty. I don't want to eat her.

"Eat. Eat. Eat. Eat." Clenching my jaw, I force the repetition from my brain. I'm here for information about my brothers, not to watch the gentle, hypnotic rise and fall of Dr. Bell's chest. I crouch, leaning some of my weight onto the mattress.

Up. Down. Up. Down. Up. Down. I have the strangest urge to rest my cheek on her chest and listen to the steady thump, thump of her heart claw at me. I don't fight the impulse to slide my hand toward her head, swirling a strand of dark hair around my glove-covered finger. Her raven hair blends with the dark material of the gloves sheathing my hands.

I could make her my doll. I rub the lock of hair against my mask, wishing I could feel the silky texture sliding across my face. She smells nice, and she's pretty. I think my mom would like her.

"Take!"

"No," I growl at nothing, causing Dr. Bell's lips to twist into a frown, rolling away from me with a huff, hair sliding from my grasp. An ache takes up space beneath my ribs. Rising from my crouched position, knees popping, I war with the indecision swarming me, buzzing like the bees that feasted on Dr. Moore's puffed-up corpse. To take her is to doom her to death. I can't let her live after I bring her to Daniels' Manor. The voices won't let me.

"Zaiden," Dr. Shaw admonishes lightly. Wise eyes tunnel beneath my skin, scraping me raw, but judgment never enters the green pools.

"The voices do not command you. You command them. Find ways to mute them. Tell me about your mom. Talking about her always distracts you."

I shake the memory loose with an agitated growl, cutting the noise short when Dr. Bell makes another noise of discontent.

To take or not to take her. I'll need to bring her with me, eventually. A month of tracking her patterns, memorizing the faces of her coworkers, and following them led me no closer to my brothers than six months ago, when I didn't even have a lead other than a name.

Zachary Lasher.

A former CEO of a merger and acquisition company, murdered in cold blood by his eldest son, Xavier Lasher. A blurry snapshot in a crumpled newspaper clipping is all I have of Zaine Lasher and his mother, Elizabeth. Zaine rarely makes public appearances, conducting meetings virtually from his secretive home address. None of the employees I'd questioned knew where the low-profile millionaire lived.

"Take her with us."

"Touch her. Taste her."

My hands grip my head, applying pressure, attempting to shove the voices out by brute force. I drop them in defeat, the clamor never ceasing. I'll need all of my mind if I'm to take Dr. Bell. But it won't be tonight. Sighing, I give the raven-haired beauty one final look before creeping out of her bedroom.

Raven.

"While I nodded, nearly napping, suddenly there came a tapping," a melodic voice whispered in his ear, bringing fingers up to tickle his belly, laughter erupting from me. His mother smiled down at him, an odd gleam in her eyes.

"Don't listen to them, Zaiden. Don't listen to the voices. The ravens are liars."

I remember her grip tightening that night, leaving bruises and the fat tears dripping down her face the next day when she saw them in the morning light. The heels of my hands dig into my eyes, forcing the memory at bay. The past keeps swiping talons at me the deeper I fall into the search for my brothers. If I didn't know any better, madness lurked at the end of this quest, razor-sharp teeth flashing in the darkness, lying in wait. It claimed my mother long before the cancer did.

I force heavy limbs down the stairs of Dr. Bell's home.

Raven. She reminds me of a raven with her long hair flowing across the pillow.

"The ravens are liars."

"Are they, Mother?" I whisper into the night air, locking the door behind me with the master key I'd made earlier in the week.

I hope my mother is mistaken like she was on a lot of things. Dr. Bell remains my only link to the remaining family I have left, just out of reach.

"Find your brothers, baby," Morgan Daniels whispered to me in her last days.

"I will, Mama," I let the night air snatch at the words, carrying them to my mother's ghost. My legs pound into the pavement, striding down the dark streets, blending into the shadows.

SARAH

I bolt upright, a scream trapped on the tip of my tongue, begging for release. Air catches in my lungs. Tears drip down my cheeks. My head droops and dark hair falls to curtain my face. I'm home. Cotton slides beneath the palm of my hands.

A shrill sound shatters the quiet. I reach for my cell phone with trembling hands, sniffing back tears.

"H-hello?" I croak, closing my eyes.

"You had a bad dream, didn't you?" Nat asks, voice lacking censure. I nod, even though she can't see it, tears continuing a steady stream. Only Natalia knows about my night terrors. They started during college, after campus police discovered my roommate had been raped and murdered in our dorm. It could've been me. Melatonin,

Ativan, and Ambien in a healthy rotation keep the worst of it at bay.

I haven't had an episode since Lauren finished college, my anxiety running rampant as long as she lived on campus. My lips won't move, refusing to confess to Natalia that the cause of the episode is the persistent feeling of eyes watching me. Similar to when police found Lauren and returned her home from the clutches of Xavier, Natalia will camp in my house like I did for Lauren, acting as honorary bodyguard.

"I'm coming over. Make room. You don't have to get out of bed. I'll use my spare and we'll chill together. How does that sound? Have you spoken to Lauren?" Dread spikes through me at having to tell my sister about the criminal that's claimed my daughter's heart.

A headache pulses behind my eyes. An insurmountable distance used to yawn between Natalia and me as kids. It took years for us to grow as women and rekindle the relationship our parents tarnished with their competitiveness and lack of insight into how a new child could make Natalia feel like an outsider. I don't pretend to know her struggles of growing up in a home where no one looked like her. But so much has happened in the past month. All of it threatens to throw our relationship back into the abyss.

My heart wants to say, "No, I just want to be alone," but instead, I say, "That sounds great, Nat. I'll call Lauren after I hang up." The lies slip off my tongue smoothly.

"Great! I'll bring coffee. White chocolate mocha with almond milk, hold the whip?" I laugh, the sound temporarily chasing the chill in the room away. Just like my shampoo, the same one I've used for years, I order the same coffee every time. Routine grounds me. In healthcare, few things are within your control. Outside of work, I prefer the mundane. Repetition decreases the chances of surprises.

"Yeah," I tell Nat, a smile curling my lips. "My usual

sounds like heaven right about now." Sinking into the feeling of normalcy, I convince myself I have nothing to worry about, that the sixth sense warning me I'm in danger is wrong.

"I can't wait to see you," I tell my sister before hanging up the call. Sometimes, intuition is wrong. The devil isn't always out to get you.

3

CHANGE OF PLANS

ZAIDEN

I didn't mean to follow her in here. Flashing lights sting my eyes, but lowering my gaze would cause me to lose sight of Sarah. Bodies press against me on all sides as I weave a path toward my raven.

"Find the raven. Catch the raven."

Long, dark hair cascades down her back in spirals. A black dress conforms to her body, leaving one shoulder bare. Red painted lips stretch in a permanent smile. She smiled most of the night, sitting at the long wrap around table next to another dark-haired woman with skin reminiscent of toffee, sipping drinks handed to her by the individuals behind the table.

Bar. That's the word my brain struggles to find, grasping blindly in the murk of my mind. A pale hand lands on a wall, catching her weight. She's too far away! Snarling, I push firmly forward, uncaring if my hood drops to expose my face. My raven needs me! She's stumbling towards a door with a figure in a dress on it.

Bathroom. Why am I struggling to find words?

My skin itches, rippling and threatening to peel off, sloughing to the dance floor I'm cutting a path through. Why would she come to a place like this? Tonight, I'd planned to take her, sitting in my parked truck across the street from her house, gloved hands drumming on the steering wheel while the gaudy pink front door glared at me accusingly, daring me to enter.

The plan changed when she bounced out of the door with that brown-skinned woman, arms linked and smiles fixed on both of their faces. They looked exuberant under the moonlight kissing their skin. And now I've lost my bird, black hair disappearing into the marked door.

"Go in. Take her."

I don't. My head bows, and I tilt my face into the fabric of my hood. I'd planned on her being unconscious when I cart her out of her home, forsaking a mask in favor of feeling cool night air brush my face. The wall I lean against undulates, rippling like disturbed water. Closing my eyes doesn't shut out the voices or the music blasting in the overcrowded space, but it does shut out the visual hallucinations taunting my mind.

In the facilities where I spent most of my youth, I rarely suffered visual apparitions. No, my mind attacked itself with whispered voices, stoking the flames of paranoia until the staff had no choice but to strap me down, forcibly injecting a sedative and antipsychotic to calm me and the demons.

"My sister is waiting for me at the bar, so please release my arm," a melodic voice floats to me beneath the layers of sounds overstimulating my senses. Sarah.

"Raven. Grab the raven."

Abandoning my perch, I stalk toward the darkened hall leading to the bathroom my Sarah just exited. A man has his hand wrapped around her arm, fingernails denting her pale flesh.

"Kill him."

On rare occasions, I agree with the voices. This time, we form an alliance. Red bleeding into my vision, I narrow my gaze on the leering corpse touching my bird.

She doesn't know it yet, but Sarah is *mine*. And the first thing I'll remove from her attacker is the offending hand still clutching her arm. His screams will sound beautiful, echoing off the walls of my childhood home. Maybe I'll scream with him when I cover him in venomous snakes.

SARAH

The creep loitering outside of the women's restroom doesn't release his hold, a lecherous grin curling wet lips, tongue sliding across them while he literally salivates over me. I try jerking free again, but he holds firm, a dark chuckle slipping from his mouth. Fear trails down my spine, bringing flashing images of my college roommate's violated body splayed across her twin mattress.

"Let her go," a deep voice slithers down the hall, a hooded figure prowling toward us. I'd think I was saved, except the barely slurred words ring warning bells in my head. I've heard that speech pattern before. We're trained to recognize speech patterns in nursing school and identify their causes. Whoever the fuck just joined the party brings up flashbacks of some of my unmedicated patients diagnosed with schizophrenia.

"Go fuck yourself, freak. Me and the lady just talkin'," the creep says, tugging me against his body. I gape at him. The fucking audacity. Raising my leg, I stab down with my heel, smiling at the howl escaping his mouth, and pull my arm free. Stepping back, heart racing, I dart frantic eyes at the tall, imposing figure still approaching.

The bent-over freak snarls, tackling the hooded man to the dirty floor. Adrenaline surges, and I kick my heels off, snatching them up in my hand, poised to use them as a weapon. The taller guy laughs, hood slipping free, facial scars catching the light.

No one comes down the hall or intervenes as the scarred man brings his interlocked hands down on the back of his attacker, an "oomph" sound drifting into the air. He does it again and again before rolling over, raining punches down on the guy who'd gripped my arm, blood splashing from the battered face.

Running forward, my hands wrap around his left arm before his fist can connect with the guy's face again. He turns wild blue eyes on me, panting breaths slipping from his full lips.

"That's enough," I tell him, pulling more gently on his raised arm. He nods, tremors traveling from his arm to my fingers. Slowly, his large body eases off the laid out guy. Taking a wary step back, I watch him merely stand above my would-be attacker, shoulders lifting and falling with rapid breaths.

"Thank you," I whisper, bringing his gaze swinging toward me.

"Are you hurt?" he asks, stepping over the other guy to close the distance between us. Shaking my head, I wrap my arms around myself, fighting my own case of tremors.

A finger touches my cheek, sliding down to lift my chin until I'm left staring into pale blue eyes that could rival the snowcaps of Mount Everest. Dark lashes line the eyes peering down at me, weaving a spell that has me lifting to my toes and brushing my lips across his cheek.

Rough skin scrapes my lips. My nose slides across his

cheek, stopping when we share the same air, his exhale transforming into my inhale.

"I should go," he whispers. But he doesn't, his large palm landing on my hip, pulling our bodies flush. My lips ghost over his, a strange compulsion gripping me. If not for his interference, would I have gotten away from that guy unscathed? Or become another statistic?

Closing my eyes, alcohol swimming in my veins, I seal my mouth over his, tongue swiping soft lips. They part, allowing me entry. He walks forward, his other hand gripping my nape. My back touches rough brick, tongue tangling with his. His groans shoot straight to my core, tightening my nipples.

What the fuck is he doing to me?

Our mouths separate, faces barely an inch apart. My eyes close, forehead landing against his. This isn't me. I don't make out with guys at bars, especially guys with questionable mental stability, who look young enough to be my son. God, he's probably old enough to date Lauren if she could get over the scars. They're eerily similar to the cartoonish ones lining the Joker's face.

"My sister is waiting for me," I tell him, retreating until my head touches the wall at my back. His eyes narrow slightly, bouncing around my head.

"You don't look alike," he says in a flat tone. My eyebrows shoot up, a kernel of fear sprouting.

"How do you know that?" I ask softly, shooting a glance down the hall.

"I saw you at the bar. The bar." His lips press close, a wince pulling at his scars. Reserving my judgment since I'm alive and mostly unmolested due to his actions, I push gently on his chest. He steps back, allowing cool air to sweep in, dissipating the heat that simmered between the tight press of our bodies.

I jerk a thumb toward the bar, giving him a soft, apologetic smile. He doesn't offer a comment, taking more steps away, a gloved hand coming up to pull his hood over his dark hair.

"Do you want my number?" I blurt, digging my nails into my palm for my impulsiveness. I'm done drinking with Natalia. My tolerance is significantly lower than hers. Joker nods, and I almost slap myself for giving him that mental nickname. He probably has a perfectly normal name, like John.

Still starts with a J. I shove the thought aside, waiting for him to pull out a phone, choosing to ignore the gloves on his hands. He's flashing a dozen red flags, but my legs are still weak from his kiss. My attacker lay sprawled in his own blood, low grunts tumbling from his mouth as he tries to push himself to his feet. Karma is a bitch.

"What's your name?" I ask before rattling off my number, watching his fingers dart across the screen.

"You can call me Z," he says, putting the phone away.

That's not really an answer, my dude.

My lips don't say what I'm thinking, leaning down to pick up my discarded heels. I need to put distance between Z and the other guy, walking away with a half-hearted wave.

My skin pebbles with goosebumps. Ignoring the sensation, I seek out my sister sitting at the bar, talking to some tattooed blond with a pair of deep dimples. I try to shove the sensation of being watched away.

Z saved me, but I can't help but feel as if the pair of eyes I've felt on my skin for the past month belongs to him. Maybe the creep in the hall wasn't the only predator I came across tonight.

4
CHASING THE MOUSE

ZAIDEN

"**F**uck you! Do you have any idea who I am? I've got people lookin' for me. You can bet your ass you won't get away with this," Gerald Martin screams, spit flying from his mouth. Scales slide across my skin, Sheba making herself comfortable, coiling around my neck.

A week passed without a text from Sarah. After the incident with the wriggling worm on the examination table, I've kept closer tabs on her, rarely letting her out of my sight outside of her job.

"Wriggling worm. Squeaky squeals. Slithering snake."

I've given up checking my phone every thirty minutes, letting the voices whittle away at the small flame of hope that the kiss she gave me meant something. My lips still tingle from her touch. My first kiss, soured by the memory of Mr. Martin's hand wrapping around her arm.

"She's forgotten about you."

"No one will look for you," I say, conserving my energy and not raising my voice to carry. I stand near the door and stick to the shadows. Sheba coils tighter around my neck and shoulders, the vibration of my voice reverberating into her reptilian underbelly. I trail a finger down the flat of her head, enjoying the scrape of scales, the difference in texture bringing a smile to my face.

Few things "ease" me, but I've always felt a kinship with insects and reptiles, as if we speak the same tongue, madness loosening mine. My collection grows each week, discovering new and exotic species. The flutter of their wings, scrape of their scales, it quiets the voices to a low murmur, like background static. Today, Sheba and I will try a new exercise, called chase the mouse.

My boots strike the tile floors, the sound ricocheting off the walls. Such beautiful acoustics in this room. Rattling of cuffs, metal grating from the erratic movements of Mr. Martin when I step into the light.

"You! Fucking freak. You broke my damn nose." My head tilts, allowing Sheba to slither higher. Did I break his nose? The moments between witnessing his hand on Sarah and the first brush of her lips against mine are a blur.

But I recall with vivid clarity swiping his wallet, walking to my truck and sitting in it, waiting for the battered, bleeding man to exit the bar. He'd staggered out with the help of security, fumbling his way to his truck. After marking his license plate, I followed Sarah and her sister home before backtracking and securing the snake food glaring up at me.

Sheba's hungry. I've kept him in this soundproof room for a week, gassing him each night and shoving a tube down his throat and pumping food into his stomach to keep him alive while withholding Sheba's meals until now. Gently, I pull her coiled form from around my neck.

Hissing, she twists her body around my forearms, refusing to settle atop of the writhing man. Clucking my tongue at her affectionately, I lower my arms until they're resting directly on Mr. Martin.

"Please! Get that fucking thing away from me. I don't like snakes." Sniffles, tears, and a patter of liquid follow the impassioned plea. Glancing between his pinned legs, I note the stain spreading across his pants. Sheba hisses, sliding off me, coiling near his head.

"Good girl," I coo, turning my back on them to the glass enclosure housing a litter of baby mice, eyes barely open. An online article says it's more humane to feed preserved dead rats to snakes. Sheba's much too intelligent for that, abandoning the meal without a second glance when I tried following those guidelines. She's a picky eater, preferring live prey, envenoming them before swallowing them whole.

"Come on, man. If this is about the girl, I wasn't going to hurt her." My body stills, nostrils flaring at the lies fumbling off his tongue. Liars. When did we stop cutting their tongues out as punishment?

"Ravens are liars."

No, Mama, Mr. Martin is a liar. Malice oozed from him in that darkened hall, pouncing on my raven like an animal gripped by a feeding frenzy. Without hesitating a moment more, I scoop out two mice, brushing their fur with my thumbs. Sheba coils, twisting and writhing next to Gerald, scenting her meal. My girl will have to work for it.

I approach Mr. Martin's head, cupping the mice in one hand and squeezing his mouth open with another. His struggles renew, face jerking side to side. I don't wait for an opportune moment, tossing one of the mice down.

Sheba strikes and Gerald screams. Mouth stretched wide, teeth buried in Mr. Martin's face, she closes the lower half of her mouth, swallowing the mouse. She undulates, retracting her teeth, and her long tail forms a barrier bracketing his head. Her slitted pupils focus on the remaining portion of her meal.

With a wink and a smile, I drop the other one into Mr. Martin's open mouth. Quick as ever, Sheba shoots into the open cavern, chasing the mouse, tail disappearing the farther she slithers down his throat. His entire body jerks up and down, eyes leaking blood. Maybe in another life, he'll think twice before touching what isn't his.

Paralyzed with a snake and mouse sliding down his throat, wide, terror-filled eyes latch onto me, silently pleading for mercy.

"Show no mercy."

I close his mouth for him, using a free hand to snatch up a blade. If possible, his eyes widen further. It's possible for Sheba to bite her way out, but that's no way to treat a treasured pet. I'll have to cut my girl free. Starting at an approximate point below the sternum, I slice down, cutting through the material of his shirt. His naked flesh wasn't something I wanted to look at for a week straight, so I'd left him clothed.

Pale flesh glows, beckoning my blade. My eyes land on the bulge in his throat. No, it's best I start there. With the paralytic venom, he shouldn't feel a thing. Positioning the tip of my blade below the chin, my hand applies pressure, blood welling from the cut. Holding his head steady with my free hand, I cut straight down, pressing deeper when I don't immediately see muscle and sinew.

When the rippling column of his throat is visible, I lessen the pressure on the scalpel's sharp edge. It appears I'll have to get my hands dirty. Discarding the scalpel, I shove one hand inside the deep cut, trailing a finger down, following the trail of Sheba's tail until I reach her head. I punch through the thin barrier separating me and my beauty, letting her twist and slither up my hand, sliding along my forearm. After she coils most of her tail around my arm, I lift my hand free of Gerald Martin's esophagus.

Her tongue flicks out, silently admonishing me. She's right. That was a cruel punishment for her. Now she's coated in blood, scales in need of scrubbing. I don't spare

Mr. Martin another look, striding out of the room with Sheba slithering around my neck. After I've cleaned my beauty, it's time for me to capture a raven.

SARAH

I have a stalker, and I'm pretty sure his first initial starts with Z. Nibbling my lip, I stare at the unopened box in my palm. It's small. My thumb rubs back and forth across the decorative cardboard. The stalker—or secret admirer since they haven't left threats at my door, just unwanted gifts—has dropped off a package on my doorstep every day for the past week. Ever since I kissed Z in the darkened hall of Louie's Bar. Taking a deep breath, I nod to myself, deciding to rip the proverbial band-aid off.

One flick of my thumb sends the lid popping off, falling in my lap. Jumping to my feet, trembling hands drop the box. An innocuous key rolls across the floor. The key to my backdoor. I thought I'd misplaced it. The receipt for the new lock and key rests on my bedroom dresser on top of the unopened box, forgotten in the whirlwind of events that's happened in the past week.

Dr. Moore's wife reported him missing. No one has heard from Dr. Anders. The ever-present feeling of being watched daily, heightens my paranoia and night terrors. Each morning, I wake up with a scream trapped in my throat.

Z. It has to be him. He watched me at the bar. Sitting down and pressing my fingers into my closed eyes, I think back over the past month, inspecting each interaction I had with strangers. But I work in a fucking hospital. I see strangers every day. Was he a patient of mine?

The temptation to call the police grips me, but I have zero evidence aside from a hunch and a lone message that says, "This is Z," after I gave him my number. Stupid, stupid, stupid move, Sarah, I admonish myself, hands slapping my forehead.

Maybe I can text him and ask him to leave me alone. Or—

Before the thought can fully form, my hand snags my phone, pulling up the text message from Z and typing two words. Only after a moment's hesitation do I press send. If he responds—No, I shake my head, changing my thought pattern.

If things escalate then I'll contact the police and inform Natalia I'll need to stay with her until my "admirer" moves on to someone else.

5
SARAH

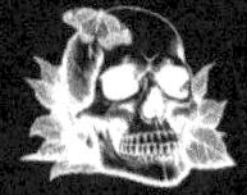

ZAIDEN

I know.

She knows. Her one word message played endlessly in my thoughts all day since receiving it. Now, beyond a shadow of a doubt, is the time for action. To take. Like a moth to a flame, my eyes find her.

Her voice sounds like music and her laughter is like trickling water, soft and whimsical. She turns, waving at a coworker, dark hair blowing across her face. Slender legs stride away from the automatic glass doors of the hospital. She's walking toward me, head down. I wonder what she's thinking as she speeds away from her place of employment, keys jangling in her hands.

"Take. Take. Take."

For once, the voices are correct. Tonight is the night I take Dr. Bell. Excitement thrums through me, flooding my limbs with adrenaline. I'm not just excited to have her at

Daniel's Manor. I'm excited about the chance to observe her up close and personal for as long as I want. It took a month of preparation, but her room is ready.

Blood rushes to unexpected places as I stalk toward Dr. Bell's stooped figure. Perhaps she keeps her head down in the vain hope of evading predators. But everything about Dr. Bell calls to me, her faint vanilla scent wafting on a gentle wind. It makes my mouth water.

"Excuse me, Doctor," I call out, pausing in a darkened section of the parking lot, hoodie covering my head. Before she turns around, I yank the edges forward, ensuring it fully obscures my mask. Dr. Bell turns a cautionary glance my way without stopping.

"If you need help, the hospital is right behind you. I'm sorry, but I'm off the clock," she says. I sway to the side, her voice striking out like a physical touch, caressing my senses. I think I could fall asleep to the sound of her voice.

"Thank you, Doctor," I say, words crawling from a dry throat. I turn as if to leave, striding toward my pickup. Her relieved sigh floats to me, the wind acting as a messenger. My lips curl upward, leaning my body against the hood of my car, facing the hospital.

Buzzing teases my ears. I swat at nothing, knowing it's in my head. Dr. Moore's ghost taunts me, but his death was not in vain. The good doctor helped me obtain paralytics, which I used to coat the door handle of Dr. Bell's car and the leather of her driver's seat.

My eyes scan the parking lot. I won't let another predator swoop up my raven. No, she's coming with me.

The buzzing grows louder and I turn, catching sight of Sarah Bell slumping down in her seat through the glass of her front windshield.

It's time to fly home, little raven.

"**S**he's awake. Look how pretty."
"Taste."
"Take."

I watch Dr. Bell squirming like a rat in a cage. Double-sided glass provides me with the perfect view of my raven, hands tugging uselessly at her restraints. She will be here a while. She should get comfortable.

"Never let her go."

My fingers press two buttons. One changes the pitch of my voice, and the other turns on the mic and two-way speakers.

"Good evening, Dr. Bell. Please get comfortable. I'm afraid your stay will be a long one." End. Her mouth opens, no doubt letting loose a hair-raising scream. She's feisty, but she'll break. And when she does, I will crack open her insides and take a peek at her secrets.

"Break. Break. Break."

She knows my brothers, the Lasher twins. Xavier remains an escaped fugitive, supposedly on the run with Dr. Bell's daughter. But where is he? How can I get close to the other one, Zaine?

"You'll never get close to them."

Sarah Bell holds the answer to these questions and until she breaks, spilling her guts, she will remain my guest. A glance at my watch reveals time crept past noon. Lunchtime.

"You'll fail."

Growling at the voices, my scars itch. I can't argue with ghosts. I need to feed my guest. My lips stretch into a grin, the scars on the corners itching with irritation. *It's time to eat, Sarah.*

SARAH

Blood rushes through my veins, and my blood pressure rises. Tears burn my eyes, but I won't give the fucker the pleasure of seeing me cry. Three-point restraints keep me pinned, one for each ankle and one on my left wrist, attached to a steel bar running the length of the wall. Fluorescent lights overhead wink intermittently, bringing to mind the articles I read about sun therapy in Alaska.

Large, square tiles cool my overheated flesh through my clothing, the black scrubs I wore to work before everything went dark. A stranger approached me in the parking lot, and then... I don't remember, trying in vain to pillage my memories, letting out a frustrated scream when I come up empty.

"I hope your dick rots off!" I yell into the four-by-four room. It reminds me of a deconstructed men's bathroom, all the stalls removed, a lone urinal glaring at me from the opposite wall. The steel bar tethering me and the urinal act as the only decorations in the room.

A rusted metal green door serves as my only symbol of escape. Cameras wink in each corner of the ceiling and spanning the length of the wall on my left, rests an onyx mirror, no doubt another form of surveillance. My free hand lifts to give him the middle finger.

I won't go down easy, mentally filtering through pressure points I can hit, major arteries begging for puncturing, and of course, if I can get enough height with the ankle restraints to kick him straight in the balls.

My head thunks against the wall behind me, minutes ticking into who the fuck knows. First, my daughter gets taken by that animal, and now this. Either Z or Xavier is behind this. And if it's Xavier, that fucker will rue the day he touched Lauren when I get free.

If, whispers a voice in the back of my mind, flashing statistics. *Fuck that.* It's too early to give up. All I can do is wait. I'm ready to meet the devil. And I'm betting he has blue eyes.

6
FOOD

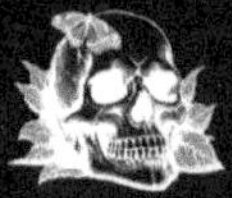

ZAIDEN

"Feed. Feed. Feed"

A wet sloshing sound disturbs the quiet, wiggling worms sliding from my palms. I catch what I can, dropping them into the blender of milk, protein powder, yogurt, and crushed Ativan. Bringing a dirt covered finger to my lip, I debate additional ingredients. Shrugging my shoulders, I internally say "fuck it", turning away from Dr. Bell's dinner, ignoring the shadows dancing on the walls in the shape of worms..

I pivot to the kitchen island behind me, a corpse resting on the slab, unseeing eyes fixed on the ceiling. My eyes follow his, not seeing what he sees, obviously. Death is such a curious thing, a gripping fascination I can't shake. I swipe a knife from the counter, brushing aside the escaped larvae.

My stomach grumbles, reminding me I've been so busy prepping for my guest I've skipped dinner. I grab a fistful of worms, popping them into my mouth, enjoying the juicy squelch they make with each bite, closing the distance between me and another ingredient for Dr. Bell.

My hand pulls up the dead man's shirt, pausing when I swear his mouth moves. My hands jerk back when his neck turns, sightless eyes narrowing on me. Pressing my hands into my eyes, I whisper, "Not real. Not real. Not real."

"She'll escape, you know. What will you do when she finds out what you did?" the dead man asks. What the hell was his name? The one before Dr. Moore, the one briskly walking toward my raven, coffee cup in hand each morning. I didn't take him for information about Dr. Bell. No, rage and jealousy churned in my veins at witnessing his "accidental" brushes against my raven.

Mine?

"*Ours,*" the voices murmur in unison, drowning out the dead man. My hands fall away, chest heaving, and I see the corpse is just a corpse, face aimed at the ceiling. Good.

"If she escapes, I'll put her downstairs. But you can't have her, not in life and most certainly not in death," I say, hand swiping a knife off the counter behind me. I point it at Dr. Anders—that was his name.

"She's mine. And you'll feed her," I growl, stalking forward with purpose, resuming the task of exposing his stomach.

A cow liver can deliver as much as twenty-one grams of protein. A human one has to be superior, and Dr. Bell needs her strength. Two scoops of protein powder add forty grams to her dinner. The beetle larvae adds another twenty-one. At eighty grams of protein, I've provided her with half her daily intake in one serving.

"*Yes, feed the raven.*"

"*Worms for the bird. Bird. Bird. Bird.*"

Blood pools around the blade, serrated edges dragging the skin down, exposing viscous fat. My knife makes a return trip, cutting through fat and viscera, blood spilling out the sides of my incisions. It's not surgical grade, but the patient offers zero complaints. I shake the sensation loose of his eyes watching me. Maybe I should've plucked them out.

His pale organs gleam at me. I shove eager hands inside the hole of the dead man's stomach, fingers trailing over familiar landmarks until I reach my prize, the human liver. One hand pulls free with a sucking sound, retrieving the blade and sawing through the attached blood vessels and intestines until the liver slips free of its tethers, landing in the abdomen's corner.

"Please don't do this man," Dr. Anders pleads, a tear leaking from his white eyes. I ignore him.

Leaving the knife inside the cavern of the corpse, I lift out the liver. Without flashing teeth, my lips lift into a small smile, the corners stopping at my cheekbones.

"She'll hate you!" Dr. Anders screams at me, hands coming to cup the open hole in his abdomen. Jerky, pale hands begin yanking out more organs, throwing them carelessly to the floor, all the while staring at me accusingly.

With one finger, I point at him, clutching the liver in my other hand. "Stay fucking dead. Leave Sarah to me. My raven!" I yell at him. Turning away, I rush to drop the freshly harvested liver into the blender. My eyes dance around and, not finding anything suitable to add nutritional value, I place the lid on top, pressing *puree*.

A whispered "Fuck you" from Dr. Anders gets drowned out by the machine. Shaking my head, I walk to the sink, rinsing my hands. She won't miss him, anyway. She'll thank me. I'm providing for her. That's right, provider. Leaning my weight on the counter, I take calming breaths, forcing my heart rate to slow.

I have a guest to feed.

SARAH

I wake with a jolt, a scream teasing the tip of my tongue. Realization dawns, eyes roaming over the masked man near the door. He stands with his hands clasped in front of him, a golden snake wrapped around his shoulders and neck, its coiled tail ending at the waistband of black pants.

Licking dry lips, I come to the startling conclusion that he drugged me. That's the only explanation for why I was awake one minute, plotting my escape, and unconscious in the next.

I didn't wake when he opened the door, assuming his perch or when he—my eyes land on the table that definitely *wasn't* there earlier—dragged the table in. Shadows cling to him, aided by his all black clothing. He tilts his head, assessing me as I assess him, appearing completely unbothered by the serpent constantly shifting across his torso.

I've been at the bedside of a known serial killer before. I didn't show fear then and I won't show it now. Even if the snake wrapped around him is potentially venomous.

"Who the fuck are you, and what do you want?" I snap, trying to control my breathing.

One hand—a spiderweb tattooed on the back—dips into a pocket, pulling out a black device similar to a recorder. A slender finger presses a button before he speaks. A voice changer, I realize, before his voice fills the room.

"Good afternoon, Dr. Bell. I have food prepared for you and it is in your best interest to consume every. Last. Drop." His boot covered feet take a step with each word as his free hand motions to a shaker bottle near my unshackled one.

Fear skitters down my spine as I wrap my fingers around the innocuous bottle. Drugged. Chained. And who knows what else he has planned?

"Please," I beg, switching gears. *Maybe I should play on being a woman? I can do that, right?* After all, if he's Z, then on some level he's attracted to me, returning my kiss at the bar.

"Mister, you have the wrong woman. I'm a mother and I—"

"Yes, adopted mother to a Lauren Bell," he finishes for me. Shock mingles with the fear in my veins. I blink unshed tears away, commanding them not to fall. So he's working for Xavier. A stalker wouldn't be concerned about my daughter if I'm their obsession. I trusted Xavier to an extent. If he cared for Lauren, then why the fuck would he have me kidnapped?

I can't help but wonder, who's the hired muscle? And he's definitely male. There's no hiding those broad shoulders, vascular hands and Adam's apple. The color black can do a lot of things—make people appear thinner—but it can't disguise the opposite sex.

"Did you hurt her?" I gasp out, my hand flying to my chest. That little girl who demanded very little, withdrawn and quiet in the first days, wrapped both hands around my heart. I cannot lose her, not like this.

Caught in my distress, I didn't hear him approach, eyes fixated on the black biker boots. I jump back when he kneels, bringing his eyes level with mine through the mask on his face.

Plastic molded into the shape of sharp cheekbones, a sinister toothy grin, and eye hole cutouts, showing startling blue eyes looking into mine. His eyes trap me, blocking out the vision of the serpent coiled around him.

It occurs to me they look eerily familiar, like staring into the eyes of Satan's twin. Instinctively, I know this man is neither Zaine nor Xavier Lasher. There's a wildness to him they lacked, his pupils jumping.

Is he Z? And what the fuck does he want with me?

If he's anything like the twins, I'm so fucked, caught in the snare of a psychopath.

7
EAT

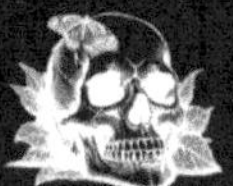

ZAIDEN

She's as pretty as I remember , wide eyes racing across my mask. Hair dark as midnight reflects the low recessed lights in the ceiling. Alabaster skin that stains with color easily, giving away more than she thinks. Firecracker. Like those black cat fireworks I used to set off in my room, causing the smoke alarm to blare. My lips turn down, remembering that eventually those couldn't wake my mother up anymore.

"Mom," I cried, shaking her unconscious form. "Please, wake up. I need you to wake up."

Blinking the fragmented memory away, I refocus on Dr. Bell's eyes. They draw me in the most, deciding that green that rivals grass is my new favorite color.

"Beautiful," I croak, bringing a hand to touch a section of hair resting on her shoulders. She jerks away from me, reminding me I spoke without turning the voice changer on. *Fuck.* Maybe she's a witch.

With my free hand, I push the button on the voice

changer while the other floats in the air, still yearning for a brush of her dark strands.

"Drink the shake, Dr. Bell," I order her, steeling myself. If she doesn't obey, she'll need to be punished. She'll learn the rules. Eventually.

"Break her."

"Feed her."

A stubborn tilt lifts Dr. Bell's chin and her emerald eyes narrow on me. Her defiance send bloods flowing faster, pooling below my waist. Fighting the instinct to look down, I grit my teeth, not commenting on her visual refusal, and waiting for the next words out of her pouty lips.

"Fuck you," she enunciates, pink lips puffing out dramatically. Oh, she's a hellcat, alright. She can't see the smile beneath my mask, sweat dotting my brow and dripping down my hoodie. If she won't eat willingly, then I'll have to connect a fucking tube and feed her that way.

"Feed. Feed. Feed."

Shut up, I command the voice repeating phrases in my head.

Hindsight's a bitch and I blended Sarah's food for this very scenario. Rising to my feet, sorrow tugs at my heart. Not even the delicious drag of Sheba's scales across my neck could dull the ache.

A part of me truly wishes she'd cooperate. But in time, she'll see things my way. Never breaking eye contact, I take a step back. And another. And another until the door touches my back.

"Don't leave her. Stay."

"Play."

Her nostrils flare every step, eyes cataloging everything. Dr. Bell is an intelligent woman. All of her colleagues said the same when I questioned them, patiently waiting for their answer and for them to take their last breath. A gas mask adorned my face as I pumped carbon monoxide into the very room she's sitting in now. Dr. Moore and Dr. Anders were the exceptions, earning a different death from their colleagues.

Turning my back on her, fully expecting her to throw her meal at me, I wonder if she can feel the ghosts of her coworkers in the room as I lock the deadbolt behind me.

SARAH

I eye the red tinted smoothie critically. Nothing suspicious about it jumps out immediately, but I can't trust a guy in a fucking skull mask who kidnaps women. My instincts scream its poison, but a sixth sense warns me if I don't drink it willingly, he'll find another way, and I'm not sure I want whatever is behind door number two.

I pick up the bottle, lean closer to my bound hand so it can pinch my nose, and I chug, throwing it back like Fireball. Memories surge of that night, the soft press of Z's lips, the warmth of his hand on my hip, fingers pressed into my neck.

I snort a laugh. I must be sick for reminiscing about the guy who more than likely kidnapped me. Some of the thick smoothie splashes on my chin and drips onto my collar. Oh, well, I keep swallowing down the strawberry-flavored smoothie.

A full feeling settles in my stomach less than halfway through the thick drink, so I set the bottle down between my legs. I look around at my pitiful surroundings and wonder if this is the moment I should pray. Death stalks every corner of life, but you see it more often in healthcare.

Jaded, I turned from my faith a long time ago, not even

bothering to raise Lauren in the church like my mother did for me. Tears swim in my eyes, clouding my vision. I sniff them back, hoping against everything that my baby girl is safe, and that Xavier didn't prove me wrong.

Two minutes. Two minutes is all it took to sum up his personality and to see the appeal Lauren saw. That fanatical, obsessive gleam in his eyes acted like a flame to a moth —my daughter. My chest constricts with all the things left unsaid between us.

I can't help but wonder if I did the right thing, leaving her with him, but the sounds coming from their room left little to the imagination. The kisses and touches she returned in front of me painted a more vivid picture than words ever could.

If the masked bastard harmed Lauren, I pray Xavier finds me and kills us both. Her light, her warmth, her smiles that greeted me every morning that I put in the effort to chase the shadows from her eyes, were my everything. I do not want to be in a world she isn't in.

Staring at my shackled ankles, the room wavers, feeling as if I'm sinking into my thoughts, threatening to drag me under. I fight the feeling, eyes widening when I realize it's a familiar sensation. Ativan. Slumping against the wall, I recall feeling this before, déjà vu attacking me.

Fuck. He did drug me.

8

TASTING HER

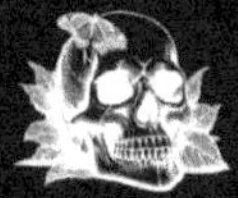

ZAIDEN

My feet trudge up the stairs, wood creaking beneath my weight. Dr. Bell continued to sleep well past three hours, her pixelated form on the surveillance cameras calling to me. Resisting the voices demanding I go to her, I decided her slumber signaled I should join her and get some shuteye as well. Separately, of course.

Pieces of wood crumble beneath the hand I trail along the bannister. I should fix that, now that I have company.

"We're here. Quit ignoring us."

"Your mother wants you to join her."

The dilapidated two story, five-bedroom home belonged to my dead mother. My eyes look up and down the hallway, walls blackened by an old fire. In a fit of hysteria, she became convinced the house was evil, deciding to douse it in gasoline and light a match. She forgot she'd left me sleeping in her bed.

"Did she forget?"

"Maybe you should've burned."

The sound of my boots striking the old wood chases away the chill of my mother's ghost and the voices taunting me. Her pall always shrouds me, and I keep myself busy to avoid falling into that well of despair. Dr. Bell is here now. She can help me keep the dead at bay, all while leading me to my half-brothers.

Pushing open the bedroom door I'd claimed as mine—not the one I used to share with my mother—I glance around, meeting the eyes of Red and Blue. They grin at me, gesturing with their hands to enter and close the door. I pull it shut, darting my eyes around for Little Brother, but he's nowhere in sight, causing a sadness to bloom within me.

Red speaks first, lips stretched wide in a mimic of the Joker. The three of us share the same scars, extending nearly to our earlobes.

"Mom, look!" I shout, ignoring the blood staining my collar, racing down the hall to her room, throwing the door open.

I pause, tilting my head and dropping the knife. The man on top of her jumps off, staring at me wide eyed.

"Oh, my God, Zaiden! What have you done?" she screams, scrambling off the bed and rushing toward me. The strange man in the corner makes my fingers itch to pick the knife back up. Instead, I turn to my mom, letting my lips pull up into a bloody smile, the pain not bothering me.

"Mom, why so serious?" My hands come up to cup her face. "Let me put a smile on that face." Horror descends over her features, pale skin whitening to an alarming color.

Red shatters the memory, rising from his crouch on the floor.

"She's here. Why are you up here with us? Go be with her." I scowl at his words, bringing my hands up to pull the hot mask off, tossing it to the floor. I want to be with her, craving it with every molecule of my body. But she'd never

accept my touch now that I've plucked her from her life. But before I can say that, Blue speaks up, abandoning his position on the edge of my bed to walk toward me.

"He's right, double-walker. Go downstairs. Taste her. She'll like it, you'll like it," he urges me.

I shake my head, dark hair brushing my forehead. They crowd around me, vultures ignoring my warnings.

"I do not know how," I snap out, eyes shifting away from the twin images of myself. Another voice, buried beneath the sins of my victims, urges me to look into a mirror and see that Red and Blue aren't real.

Red talks over that voice, aloud and echoing in my mind.

"Taste her," he growls, hands clenched at his side. Blue shifts to stand near my right shoulder, eyes a twin to my own peer into mine.

"Taste her," he repeats after Red. Soon, they're both chanting it.

"Taste her. Taste her. Taste her. Taste her. Taste her."

Clapping my hands over my ears cannot drown them out.

"Fine!" I scream at ghosts, opening eyes I'd forgotten I closed. I am alone.

"Fuck!" I yell at no one, snatching the mask back up and stalking out of the room, slamming the door shut, hoping the dead can't sleep if I don't.

SARAH

Something soft and slick slides against me, pulling a moan from my dry mouth. My brow furrows, trying to pull up my memories of who could possibly be between my legs. Another slow lick stalls my thinking process. My hips raise on their own, silently begging the stranger to keep licking me.

A hum vibrates against my folds, teasing my clit. A fog clouds my mind and I'm helpless against the pleasure twisting tighter and tighter with each lick. I wish they'd occur more often, and firmer. It was a tease, shoving me at the edge and keeping me there.

"Please," I mumble. My eyes weigh a ton, refusing to open to see who's licking me into the next realm. They hum again, edging me closer off the edge. My hand weighs only slightly less than my head, sliding to tangle in soft hair, pressing their face more firmly against my pussy.

"Yes," I moan when a tongue spears into me, nose pressing against my clit.

"More," I beg, abandoning all restraint, lifting my hips for every flick. Fingers dig into my thigh, spreading me open, but I didn't care. I never want them to stop, every caress stoking the flames of a fire I thought had died out long ago. Motherhood, work, and outside stressors striped away the Sarah I was before Lauren walked into my life with those brown, almond-shaped eyes.

"Yes, right there," I cry out, the tip of a tongue targeting my clit, over and over until my hips rise completely off the floor, pleasure washing over me, tightening and relaxing my limbs.

A muffled growl vibrates through me and I wish I can open my eyes to see this unknown pussy eater giving me the first orgasm I haven't given myself in over ten years. Their clothing rustles against my body and I feel them tugging at my legs.

Too tired to stop them, I wait, fabric creeping up my legs. They're dressing me. A sigh escapes me, and a familiar exhaustion reaches back for me with greedy fingers, dragging me back into darkness.

I didn't even have time to thank my pleasure partner before I'm slipping under.

9

VOICES

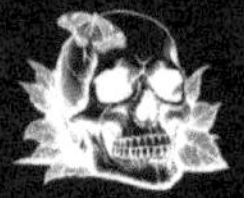

ZAIDEN

Dr. Bell passes back into slumber, eyes drifting closed with a soft smile on her face. I can't believe I did that or more accurately, she enjoyed it, liquid gushing from her to coat my chin when her body seized. My tongue passes back over my lips, collecting every drop. I could get addicted to that.

Red and Blue flank me, providing a buffer to the murmurs in my head. They silently watched as I devoured Sarah.

Sarah.

Hebrew for princess and I want to serve her on my knees any time she opens her legs. But she won't remember what just happened. I scramble to snatch my gas mask up and secure it in place, only taking a deep breath when filtered air rushes in.

Nitrous Oxide pumps into the room in a steady stream. Combined with whatever percentage of Ativan she consumed from her meal, Sarah was as docile as a lamb when I unchained her, pulled her pants down and dove into her center like a man possessed. Glancing at my doubles, I can conclude I am a man possessed, beyond any redemption if modern medicine can be trusted.

Running a final gaze over the treasure I snatched up, dark hair haloing her cherubic face, I turn to leave, Red and Blue matching my step.

The metal door I'd installed before Dr. Bell's arrival slams shut. My hands engage the deadbolt, hesitating only a moment before resuming the trek to my bedroom. Exhaustion dogs me and voices creep into my mind, demanding my attention.

By the time I make it to my room, my head swims with erratic thoughts, hands trembling. The next deadbolt I lock takes me several minutes to click into place. I toss the key into the farthest corner of the room, knowing I won't be coherent enough to find it for some time.

Sinking to the dust covered floor, hands flying up to my head, I give into the madness, letting the voices talk over each other, drowning me out until only a sliver of sanity remains.

Sarah.

SARAH

Blinking my eyes open, I'm greeted with the same fluorescent lights I fell asleep under with no concept of time. Shifting into an upright position, I note a familiar stickiness between my thighs.

No!

My free hand darts down my pants, moaning at the first brush of my fingers over my swollen clit.

He did.

Shame and arousal burn through me, but I don't stop my fingers from skating across my clit, over and over again. Pleasure crests and I'm transported back to the prior night, a gentle tongue giving careful licks. I imagine it's his tongue stroking me, bringing me to the ledge I thought I'd never stand on again.

The door bangs open and I jump, snatching my hand away, cheeks burning. Literally caught with my hand in the cookie jar.

He stalks forward, boots pounding into the floor, pulling the door closed behind him. His shoulders heave up and down, drawing my attention to the gas mask adorning his face.

Instinctively, my lungs pause their work, preventing the flow of air. The fucker is drugging me with gas and whatever he slipped into that damn smoothie. I glare at him, silently daring him to come closer. The mask only protects his face.

"Let me ease you," he rasps, voice hoarse and husky, a combination that tightens my nipples. But I've seen this movie before with my daughter as the star actress.

"Go fuck yourself," I snap, forgetting to hold my breath. My guilty hand curls into a fist and I ignore the wetness on my fingers.

"You had no right," I snarl, nails digging into my palms. It doesn't matter how good it made me feel. I never consented. My eyes stare daggers into him, daring him to disagree.

"You enjoyed it." Confusion and a glimmer of heat seep into his voice.

"That doesn't matter. You didn't ask," my finger stabs at him. "You had no right. Do not fucking touch me again." My chest heaves, heart banging against my ribs.

His head cocks, reminding me of an animal right before

they attack. My head is shaking before he even starts marching toward me.

"No!" I scream, scooting as far as my shackles allow, shaking my head and sending my hair flying around my face.

He stops less than a foot away, heavy breathing filling the air.

"Please," I beg again. "Please don't touch me."

"You liked it." He almost sounds confused, causing me to briefly wonder his age. It didn't matter. *No meant no, fucker.*

"You drugged me," I try to reason with him, breast heaving and hardened nipples scraping the insides of my bra. My feet jerks toward me when he kneels, stretching a hand toward one foot.

"Let's make a trade." I blink at him, uncertain of how I feel about the desperation lacing his words. No guy had ever *bartered* to eat me out.

"Let me go—"

"No." His hand creeps under my pants leg, wrapping slender fingers around my calf.

"Pick something else," he says, idly rubbing my skin, hand easing higher.

"I want to call my daughter." My chin lifts, daring him to refuse me when he threatened me with her.

Did he?

I push the traitorous thought aside. He mentioned Lauren while I'm chained up in the middle of who knows where. It's enough.

"Two minutes," he agrees, dragging his nails past my knee, stretching my scrubs with half his arm under the material. "No hints, no details, no code words." He leans forward, and my head thumps against the wall in a rush to evade him.

"You lie, she dies." My lips tremble with unshed tears at

the blatant threat I cannot ignore. I nod, nose tingling with the urge to cry. If hearing my baby girl's voice is all I get, I'll take it.

"After," he says, yanking me toward him until my back hits the floor.

"Close your eyes and do not look at me or the deal is off." I squeeze them closed, one hand fisted at my side and the other resting against the steel bar it's linked to.

10

A TASTE

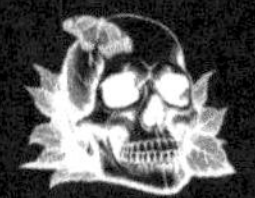

ZAIDEN

I'm ravenous, dying for a taste of her, head swimming with depraved thoughts. Before her, women never interested me. Now, I can't get enough, needing her on my tongue, sliding down my throat.

"Again. Again. Again."

"Keep her."

My fingers shake slightly, sliding a key out of my pocket. Deciding to play it safe, I unshackle one ankle first, reaching up to pull her pants down. She lifts her hips, cheeks stained an adorable red.

Why would she say she didn't like it when she clearly did?

"Because you're worthless."

"She doesn't want you."

I don't understand, but I'll make her gush again.

Ten hours. I lost ten hours to the voice in my head, waking up on my bedroom floor, sunlight stabbing into my eyes. I rushed from my room, fear gripping my heart, needing to make sure her chains kept her contained. One voice taunted, I'd lose her like my mom, that I'm destined to lose the people I care about.

One pants leg clears her feet and I'm left staring at it. *Do I care for her?*

"Yes," all of the voices whisper in unison.

A shudder travels through me, licking my lips, remembering last night. She tastes like a flavor I can get sick from consuming, souring my appetite for anything else.

"You never told me your name," she mumbles, eyes dutifully closed. I relapse the chain around her ankle, pondering what name to give her. My mother called me… No, I can't tell her that one.

"Dayton," I croak, throat still hoarse. I must've screamed the entire ten hours or something to it. But, Red and Blue were absent from my room, along with the voices, when the sun rose again.

One left to go. I unlock the cuff, pulling the rest of her bottoms off, fully exposing her lower half to me. Long slender legs, testament to the hours she spends each week working out. I learned her schedule, following her in the shadows. She worked too long hours, often getting home at night and waking up before six a.m. to do something called CrossFit.

I pull the free leg away from the other, licking my lips at her damp folds gleaming in the light. She gasps, but her eyes remain closed. My nails dig in, suddenly gripped by the desire for her to say my real name, not the middle name I gave her.

"Zaiden. Zaiden. Zaiden."

Dammit. I guess I'll have to drown my regret in the taste of her on my tongue. Eager hands rip the gas mask off, thankful for the foresight to turn the gas off before I walked in. My face darts forward, eager to swallow down every drop of wetness she produces for me.

It is all *mine*.

SARAH

A shocked cry leaves my lips, Dayton's mouth ravaging me like I'm his last meal. Gone are the careful licks from the night before. His tongue repeatedly spears my opening, slurping down my slick. Soft lips cushions my clit, rubbing back and forth while he tastes me.

Once more, one of his hands keeps my leg spread, nails digging in. His hungry groans and possessive growls send vibrations through me and I'm so close to tumbling over the edge, I could scream.

"Dayton," I moan, rolling my hips for more, needing *something* more. My hand snakes into his hair, holding him in place, my body forgetting why I was against this to begin with.

His name on my lips snaps something in him. He moves both hands to grip my hips, pulling me into his face, sucking my clit into his mouth, wrenching a long, low moan from me.

"Yes!" I cry out, shifting my hips for more, each suck winding that tension within me tighter and tighter. His teeth scrape over my clit and my head throws back, screaming as pleasure slams into me. His mouth never relinquishes my clit, sucking me in swallows, prolonging the wave into an endless stream.

I'm a twitching mess beneath him, aftershocks running through me. When the last one fades, I slump to the floor, eyes still closed.

I can't believe I let him do that. Again.

Slowly, as if reluctant, he removes his mouth from me, swallowing audibly. Tension settles between us, my ears perked, listening for whatever he does next. He promised to let me talk to my daughter. Sniffling, tears burn my eyelids.

How the hell am I supposed to talk to her after letting my kidnapper and potential stalker give me one of the best orgasms of my life?

Our last argument circled around her letting Xavier ruin her life, throwing away her career to run off to Mexico with him. I didn't condone it, voicing my objections. But Lauren's a grown woman, my protests falling on deaf ears. The more I argued against it, the more she sank her heels in, that stubborn child of mine.

Now, what do I tell her? Let's swap stories?

"Sarah?" There's a questioning note to my name and I shake my head, refusing to unburden myself to him, opening that door on Stockholm Syndrome.

"I'm fine. If you can put my pants back on and fetch a phone, that'd be great. We had a deal, after all." A sour taste coats my tongue when the words fly from my mouth, diminishing what he did to me.

But I have to stay strong. If not for me, then for Lauren.

11

PROMISE NOT TO RUN

ZAIDEN

Her words send an empty feeling unfurling in my chest. Stomach roiling, my hands blindly reach for my mask, making sure her eyes are still closed as I straighten to pull it back on. Air saws in and out of my mouth.

A quick look reveals she'd tilted her face toward the wall, away from me, worsening that sensation behind my ribs. Shadows writhe and twist on the walls, tendrils threatening to brush my raven's dark hair.

Before that happens, I re-dress her quickly, brows furrowed as I attempt to analyze the queer feeling she unlocked within me. Dr. Sarah Bell has altered my world in more ways than one, awakening a foreign hunger and igniting unfamiliar feelings.

What do I do with her?

"Keep her."

She's the key to uniting with my brothers, but I'm no longer sure I can release her. I want to hoard these new things she's exposed me to. Red and Blue are absent, offering zero guidance on what to do next.

But the shadows keep stretching along the walls, gaping maws snapping menacingly at Dr. Bell. Daniels' Manor does not want the good doctor within its walls. The walls ripple and roll in waves. Closing my eyes behind my mask and relaxing my fisted hands, I inhale and exhale slowly.

"Do you promise not to run?" I ask her, hoping she doesn't lie to me. I detest liars. She's more likely to break an ankle, her feet punching through the weak floors to land in the basement in a broken heap.

"*Ravens are liars.*" And the Daniels' are infected with madness, Mama.

Sarah's eyes pop open, a quizzical expression gracing her face.

"You're not bringing a phone in here?" she asks, almost petulantly. Did she not want to be in my presence any longer?

Relieved she can't see my face, anger flushes my skin at the hint of rejection. She enjoyed it, so why does she act like this?

"No," I snap, curling my hands into fists to avoid reaching for her, proving she enjoys my mouth. "Do you want to use the house phone or not?" I've no idea what I'll do if she refuses me. I already know I can't go without another taste of her, and accepting this bargain is an opening for it to happen again. And again. I'm hooked, wanting a taste every day of the week, imagining what I'm willing to bargain for tomorrow.

"You have a house phone?" Her eyebrows raise to her hairline. Narrowing my eyes, I try to understand why she seems shocked by that. Doesn't everyone have a house phone?

"Yes. And you can use it so long as you follow my terms

and don't try to run." A shiver of excitement runs down my spine, making me jump to my feet.

Do I want her to run?

"Yes," Red supplies, appearing out of nowhere, lounging against the wall near Sarah's head. I scowl at him, but also relief courses through me. I'm sick, but I don't want to be cured, left alone within my mind.

Red and Blue take the place of real friends, and it never bothered me until I look down at Sarah, watching her shift into an upright position, completely oblivious to my double standing near her shoulder.

SARAH

It's on the tip of my tongue to tell him to shove his phone somewhere sunless, but I bite back the words, bowing my head and letting my hair swing forward in a curtain to shield my face. I'm doing this for Lauren. At least, I tell myself that, squirming a little at the sticky sensation between my thighs. I doubt my screams earlier would convince a jury that my actions were selfless.

"Do you agree?" he asks, raspy voice skittering across my sensitive senses. I nod, knowing he can see me through his mask.

Grunting, he shuffles around, a lock clicking before metal slips free from my ankles. I wiggle them experimentally. They move without a hint of discomfort, whispering of a painless escape. But I know better, instincts screaming that the man moving to my wrist to unshackle it is dangerous and unpredictable. Something about him niggles at my intuition, a sixth sense I honed in my years of nursing.

In a hospital setting, I'd avoid ever being left alone with him, keeping the door at my back.

Metal clanks to the floor, sounding loud in the small space.

"Ready?" he asks, withdrawing a hand from his pocket to help me stand. I stare at it a minute longer than necessary. A scar, about an inch wide—perhaps the width of a blade—sits in the center of his palm, and scars and calluses decorate his fingers. My father used to ramble about how you can tell a lot about a man from his hands, from whether he uses lotion to condition his skin and is unfamiliar with labor to how many hours he spends bailing hay.

Dayton's hands look like they belong to a killer. Before I can think better of it, I slap one of my hands into his.

12
OURS

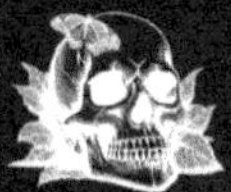

ZAIDEN

Her hand slips into mine, the impact stinging with inevitability.

"*Ours,*" Red growls, prowling closer, nose brushing through her hair. Blood splattered walls flash in my mind, and I stare at him in warning. Sarah is *mine*. I will not share her with my demons, even if they wear my face.

Tugging lightly, keeping my eyes forward, I lead my newest addiction out of her cell. My eyes drift to her frequently, gauging her reaction as we walk down the hall, floors groaning beneath our combined weight.

"Do you live alone?" There's a slight tremor in her voice. *Fear? Does she think I'll share her?*

"*Ours,*" Red and Blue intone in unison, trailing behind us. A shiver races across her, and she folds her arms over her chest, arms acting as a shield. Perhaps she can sense what she can't see. Insanity.

"*Make her like us,*" Blue suggests, breath ghosting over my neck. I fight the shudder.

Restraints clamp down on my wrists and ankles. Hands hold

me down. Tears stream down my cheeks. I scream and curse everyone present. A hand pries open my mouth. I snap my teeth at them, and they shove a piece of cloth inside, clamping a hand over my mouth to prevent me from spitting it out.

"Somebody fucking sedate him! I can't give the shock with him wriggling around," a voice booms outside of my line of sight. I fight harder, nausea climbing up my throat.

"No!" I scream, snot mingling with tears, jerking my body in every direction I can.

"You don't have more of your buddies waiting around, do you?" Sarah asks, stopping in the middle of the hallway, emerald eyes trained on me. My breathing comes fast, and I force my body to relax, re-immersing in the present. No one will ever touch me like that again. They'd have to kill me.

And I'd have to kill anyone who even thinks of performing electroconvulsive therapy on Dr. Bell.

Remembering her question, I shake my head, motioning with my hand for us to keep moving. The kitchen is just around the corner. I barely remember disposing of the body in the incinerator out back, putting choice pieces of meat on ice for her.

It's a good thing too, eyes tracking her reactions when we round the corner, and she pauses at the doorway to the kitchen. I mentally pat myself on the back for cleaning up the majority of the blood splatters from my dissection.

Wide eyes turn to clash with mine, causing my brows to rise. The kitchen is clean. *What could she possibly be upset about now?*

SARAH

He's a killer. He's a killer. He's a killer. He's a killer.

There's blood on the ceiling, splatters staining the legs of the bar stools, and aged blood catching the light is embedded in the cracks of the tiled floor of the kitchen. I'm not going in there, taking a wary step back.

I let him touch me. His mouth and murderous hands tainted my skin. Bile crawls up my throat, and I'm shaking my head. I'm going to die here.

My eyes shift to him, finding his trained on me already. His head tilts, dark hair grazing the edges of his mask. The mask obscures most of his face except those cerulean eyes searing into my soul. I don't know how I know, but I know he's not letting me go anytime soon.

"Don't show fear. Some patients are like bloodhounds. Don't let them smell it on you," Dr. Sawyer lectured, absently straightening the lapels on his white coat.

My precept words echo in my mind, and the urge to run grips me, constricting my air. Dayton steps closer, towering over me. I catch his hand out of the corner of my eye, lifting and dropping back down to his side. I stare at it, noting the pattern of scars are straight slashes across the back like someone dragged a knife across his knuckles horizontally out of boredom.

My eyes shoot back up to his.

"What do you want with me?" The unknown stretches out in my mind's eye, taunting me. I need to know.

"You're going to help me with something important. But first, I thought you wanted to use the phone." Dark brows drop low over his eyes, conveying his confusion. But something about his words and mannerisms brushes across something familiar, something I've encountered before in other patients.

"You live alone. Do you have family or friends?" I

hedge, fingers twitching at my side, nervous energy needing to be burnt off.

"Are you trying to get to know me, Dr. Bell, or manipulate me?" Menace and a veiled threat lurk in his voice. Unbidden, the phantom feeling of what it felt like to have him suck my clit into the wet cavern of his mouth surges forward. Threat or not, he's dangerous, but in that moment when he bartered to taste me, he was merely a man desiring a woman. I can use that. Because suddenly, I suspect I know what kind of animal I'm dealing with.

13
MANIPULATION

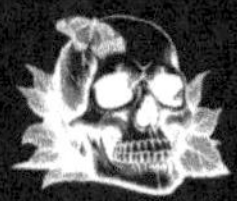

ZAIDEN

She's trying to manipulate me.

"Kill her."

I know it, but I genuinely want to share with her, tell her who I am and who I used to be. I want her to *see* me. But she won't. Nurses and doctors like her never did.

"She's just like them."

"Getting to know you," she lies, the words dripping off her traitorous tongue.

My body moves without thinking, crowding her until her back meets a wall, then wrapping a hand around her throat. She pants, showing me a hint of that tongue, nostrils flaring and pupils expanding. *Does she like this?*

My head leans closer, and I wish I could smell her through the mask.

"You're lying, Dr. Bell. I dislike liars," I warn. Her pulse throbs in my hand, either from fear or excitement, I can't tell. My mouth moistens for a taste, saliva collecting in the corners and beneath my tongue.

Red and Blue's chant from the night before stabs into my brain.

Taste. Taste. Taste.

"Tell me the truth. Why do you want to know?" I inhale deeply, hoping to catch a spare whiff of her scent through the filtration of the mask. It eludes me.

"I don't owe you anything," she snaps, fire sparking in whorls of green. Her heartbeat flutters like a butterfly against my palm, and I'm convinced it isn't due to fear.

What to do?

SARAH

Dayton's hand rests against my throat, sending signals to my pussy, dampening my panties. I don't need a mirror to know red flushes my face, and I resist leaning into his touch. A fucking gas mask lies inches from my face. None of this—the entire situation—should arouse me, but I can't wrangle my body to get the message.

"And I don't owe you anything," he snarls behind his mask, grip tightening briefly. "If you think you're going to manipulate your way out of here—" My broken laugh cuts him off, causing that curious head of his to tilt.

"You're not answering, so that means no to both. If you don't have any family, then you're either an orphan or recently lost someone, and grief makes us do stupid things. If you have no friends, it's because you have trouble making and sustaining connections, leading me to believe you have a social disorder or a mental illness that impairs your judgment, and you're probably unmedicated." I get it all out in a rush, heart racing behind my ribs and palms sweating.

He could very well kill me after this, but I'm betting on my life he has a social disorder. Hell, doctors diagnosed Jeffrey Dahmer with borderline personality disorder. If I know his diagnosis, I can understand his mind. Manipulate my way out of here? I'm trying to get him to keep me alive for as long as possible, and all I have at my disposal is my body and my mind.

Someone has to come looking for me.

14
ANOTHER KISS

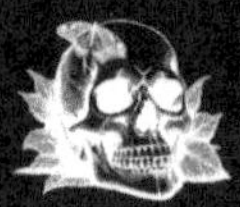

ZAIDEN

Her words are a douse of freezing water, icy tendrils abrading my flesh and mind.

Does she think I'm crazy?

"And if I am mentally ill, Dr. Bell, are you going to help me?" I ask, leaning closer, the edge of my mask brushing her face. My eyes track her flush spreading, racing down her neck, and probably staining her chest. My fingers itch to rip her shirt off and see for myself, but would that prove her right?

To be clinically insane is to be no better than an animal. A psychiatrist told me that once, sitting across from me, a straitjacket pinning my arms against my body. I was a bug beneath his microscope, and he wanted to dissect my mind. *Does Dr. Bell want the same? If I let her, will she let me taste her again?*

I lick my lips in anticipation, the question resting on my tongue. "If you're mentally ill, Dayton, then you need more help than I can provide. I specialize in pregnancy and childbirth." Her words sound earnest, possessing a kernel of empathy, warming my soul.

Can I convince her to like me? To stay willingly?

I'm almost tempted to try. But my mind conjures images of all the doctors that failed me and my mother, how thready and weak her voice got in the end, thin hand gripped in mine as I pleaded for her to stay with me, to not leave me alone.

She'd whispered, "Find your brother," on an endless loop until her last breath eased out, eyes going out of focus.

"Dayton," Sarah gasped, my fingers having tightened inadvertently around her throat, how I imagined them enclosing around the doctors that kept repeating, "We did the best we could do."

False platitudes and schemes written on their faces. They plotted to lock me up in a padded room, dragging me kicking and screaming away from my mother's still-warm body.

"D-D—" My hands jerk away from Sarah, feet ferrying me away, heart pounding in my chest. I nearly hurt her, the key to my mother's dying wish, an end to this isolation.

"Help me," I force the breathless words out. Her pupils nearly eat up the whites, taking a hesitant step forward, hand outstretched. I remain still, watching her approach, not daring to breathe.

When she stands in front of me, fingers brushing the edge of the mask curving beneath my jaw, I clamp a hand around her wrist. I can't let her see. She'll get scared, like all the others, running from me.

"Insane," Dr. Barker whispered in my ear, four-point restraints constricting my movements.

"I can't wait to see what your insides look like," he whispered, lips ghosting over the shell of my ear.

The past claws at me, digging talons into my underbelly,

scraping the axons, trying to tell me Sarah is standing right in front of me.

SARAH

His chest moves up and down in a rapid pattern, pupils expanding but staring unfocused at a point beyond my head.

Panic attack.

Heart in my throat, I do the only thing I can think of. I yank on his mask, pulling his face down. He makes an incoherent "Nnng" sound, but my fingers are scrambling to pull the mask above his jaw, exposing full lips. With part of the mask exposing his face, I grip the back of his neck with both hands, shifting my weight on my tip toes and brushing my mouth across his.

He groans, hands landing on my waist. I do it again, just as soft, a phantom caress. His lips part, panting against mine.

"Again, please," he croaks, eyes half closed. I do it again, flicking my tongue to drag along his bottom lip. His gasp is my reward, and I shove the tip of my tongue inside his mouth.

"F-fff," he grunts, letting me lead and slowly kiss into his mouth.

His lips are so soft, but the edges feel raised, like old scars. *He is Z!* Ignoring that revelation and not wanting to propel him back into whatever triggered his panic attack, I focus on the non-scarred portion of his mouth, cupid bow, and full bottom lip.

He doesn't kiss me back, breathing heavily and holding

still. Almost as if it's his first kiss. But that can't be right. We kissed at the bar. I pull back, resting my heels on the ground, and he groans, leaning down to chase my mouth.

"Please, don't stop," he begs, voice airy and choked with need. My pussy clenches on air, and I take it as a sign to stop. I kissed him merely to stop his panic attack. Nothing further needs to happen between us, and he promised me a phone call.

15
MY NAME

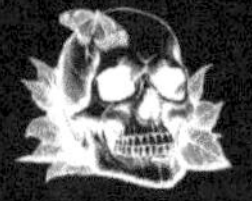

ZAIDEN

Panic lashes at me, lips tingling from Sarah's unexpected kiss. Twice now, she's kissed me. Before her, no one had ever kissed me. With my scars, I thought no one ever would and never expected to enjoy it. Raw craving rushes at me, and I *need* her.

"Sarah," I rasp, desperation creeping into my voice. "Please do that again. I'd give you anything," I beg shamelessly.

Her mouth gapes open, and the sight of her swollen lips races straight to my hardening cock. I glance down at it quizzically.

"No," she says, shaking her head, eyes trained on the erection straining my pants. She points at it like it's a weapon waiting to jump out at her.

"No, that's a step too far," her hands gesture widely, taking in the foyer we're standing in. "All of this is too far. Please, Dayton, just let me go. I know a few psychiatrists —" Cold dread skates down my spine, and I'm closing the distance before she can finish talking.

She squeaks, then gasps when I slam my mouth onto hers.

"Dayton," she gasps, but I swallow the sound down, needing more of her mouth, her sounds, everything. I want all of it, unfulfilled until I've swallowed her whole. My hands snatch at her, pulling her into my body, cock rubbing against the inside of my pants.

Will she let me put it inside of her?

My balls tighten, threatening an eruption if I continue down that train of thought. Her hands shove at my chest but grip my shirt to pull me in. I can taste her confusion mingling with her sweet surrender, moaning into my mouth.

I kiss her sloppily, hungrily, tongue swooping into every corner of her mouth. Impatient with the distance between us, I grip beneath her ass cheeks, hefting her into the air. My groan gets trapped between our tangled mouths when she wraps her legs around my waist, bringing her pussy flush with my cock.

I want inside her more than I've wanted anything. Logic tells me I'll lose her before I've gained her if I force her. It's the first time I'm keen to listen to sanity.

I pull my mouth away from hers, and she moans in frustration, hips rolling against my cock, balls tightening painfully.

"Sarah," I gasp, vision winking in and out, a tingle in my spine edging me closer to releasing in my pants.

"I want you," I confess. Her breasts rest against my chest, and I feel each inhalation she takes, silence settling between us.

"You can't keep me here, Dayton, and expect me to just sleep with you. That's not how this works. And I don't even know what you look like!" she exclaims, trailing her fingers across my scars. Facial muscles jump beneath her touch.

Can I show her?

"If I show you, will you promise not to run?" My throat constricts, struggling to swallow the extra saliva in my mouth.

"Will you promise to let me go?" she retorts, stubbornness lining her lifted chin.

Fuck! How the hell am I supposed to let her go when she's awakened desire in me for the first time?

Before her, I swore my cock was a broken, limp thing, never rising for any sort of stimuli. It's her, all of it. I might have to kill her to keep her from leaving, preserving her body like my mother's down in the basement. She'd be the most beautiful corpse. Red, Blue, and I could start a collection.

But I already know there won't be another Sarah, another awakening. She'd take all of these new things with her to the grave, further damning me in this half-existence.

My teeth grind on each other, my mind flipping through decisions, all of them ending with her leaving me.

"Dayton." I wince at the name, not for the first time wishing she'd say my real name. Closing my eyes, I come to a decision, hoping against all hope that it won't cost me the piece of treasure in my arms.

SARAH

Dayton's eyes close and I wait a beat, holding my breath, hope unfurling in my chest. When he opens them, resolve steeling the vibrant blue, I know he's not letting me go like I asked. My weight shifts back, prepared to bolt and kick and fight if I have to. The front door lies just behind me.

"My name isn't Dayton," he whispers, one hand releasing the hold on me to slide up to the edge of his mask. My heart sounds like a drum in my ear or an ocean crashing into the shore, anticipation raising hairs on my nape and arms.

"My mother," his voice cracks, lashes flurrying up and down with rapid blinks. "She named me after my dead brother. He died as a babe." His Adam's apple bobs with a nervous swallow.

My eyes latch onto the fingers, shoving this mask up and off his head, air leaving my lungs. Without thought, my fingers fly to the scars on either side of his mouth, jagged healed cuts in a fashion eerily similar to the Joker. The low light from the bar when I first saw him barely did them justice.

"Dayton. Who did this to you?" I ask, uncaring if he's a kidnapper or a murderer. It looked painful and the bumpy skin, neatly healed, implies it was done years ago. His face put him in his early twenties, practically a child to me. I can't imagine someone disfiguring him at a young age.

Every villain has an origin story. What was his?

"My name is Zaiden." He talks around my fingers rubbing back and forth over his scars. My hand jerks back instinctively upon hearing his name.

"You're a Lasher," I snarl, compassion withering up like dead weeds.

His hair flops against his ears and forehead as he shakes his head.

"Not technically. My mother slept with Zaine and Xavier's father. They met at a grief group and…" he trails off, but the picture shines all the same. A grieving father, a vulnerable woman, and then there's Zaiden several months after whenever the deed happened.

"Why tell me your name is Dayton?" I ask, latching onto that over all the things in need of unpacking. He's Xavier's half-brother. My lips twitch, wondering where the hell both of them got the kidnapping gene.

"My legal name is Zaiden Dayton Daniels." My eyes watch his scars twist and contort with his speech and facial movements. He didn't answer me when I asked who disfigured him, but as my eyes land on his, I suddenly know the answer.

It falls into place like dominoes.

16
THE NEED TO KNOW

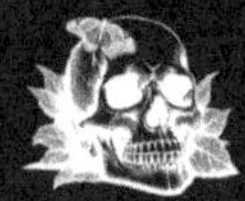

ZAIDEN

She looks at me like I'm a puzzle that she's unraveled. It feels odd but nice. No one has ever looked at me like they have me all figured out. Psychiatrists scratched their heads and threw medicine at me and my mother. Her absence is a festering hole in my chest I'm hoping my brothers can fill, or I might go more insane than I already am.

"You did this to your face," her fingers hesitantly return, and I nod. It's my hope that all this honestly will convince her to stay, to lie with me. I crave to be inside her, but a part of me would be content if she merely held me as my mother used to while petting my hair. It's a hunger that's never satiated.

"Why? Where's your mom?" Her eyes well with tears, but I'm not certain if they're for me or her since she's stuck with a madman who disfigured his face on a whim.

"I wanted to make her smile," I answer her first question, not wanting to touch the second. It's a wound barely covered with scabs. One wrong move, and it bleeds into my cerebrum, inciting the voices, tangling the lines of reality. I do not want that. I wish to be present with Sarah, my awakener.

My body comes alive in her presence, a zombie given a new lease on life. My mind wanders to her next meal. If she doesn't ask about her colleagues, then I won't tell her there are slices of them in the refrigerator.

"Level with me, Da-Zaiden," she stammers over my name. My brows raise, and I wonder if I'd like Dayton more as long as it fell from her lips.

"You can keep calling me Dayton," I reassure her, rubbing both of my hands up and down her back. I want us closer than close. If she's upset about my face, then she wouldn't agree to mix our blood or carry a piece of me with her, like my fingernail clippings or a lock of hair.

She gives me an assessing look, then firmly pushes at my chest. Gritting my teeth, I lower her to her feet, already regretting relinquishing my prize.

"What's your diagnosis?" Her words are razor sharp and blunt, an abrasion to my ears. *Why does she need to know?* My nostrils flare, and I debate not answering, but her hands land on both hips and her eyes narrow on me. Suddenly, I feel like spilling my guts and anyone else's to appease her.

"Schizophrenia," I fire back in the same clipped tone. Her head nods, face devoid of surprise. *She knew?*

"You knew?" My mind races through all our interactions. I never once talked to Blue or Red in front of her.

"I already pegged you for having a social disorder or a mental illness. It fits," is all she says, glancing away from me. If she runs toward the front door, I will put her in the same coffin with my mother for a night, giving her a taste of the nightmares that plague me in my waking hours.

"Why did you take me, Dayton? Why did you stalk me?" she murmurs softly, not looking at me.

"Your daughter is with one of my brothers. I thought you could help bridge the gap. Tell me everything you know about them. I didn't plan—" My words get trapped in my throat, and I swallow them down. Shaking my head, I know she won't want to hear that.

"You didn't plan what?" she asks, eyes on me. Gulping, I nod, forcing myself to spit the words out.

"I didn't plan—" Nausea twists in my gut. I can do this. "I didn't plan to taste you." My tongue licks my lips nervously, and I keep going. "I didn't plan for you to give me my first kiss." Red washes across my face at that admission, but surely, she has to know? That she's the first. The first of everything.

"I didn't plan on wanting to keep you after I've gotten everything I needed from you. But I do. I want you here, Sarah, for good." My eyes search hers, but shutters shield her emotions from me. I want to tear them down. She should hide nothing from me.

SARAH

The floor drops from beneath me, and vertigo assails me, snatching at my limbs.

Dayton wraps both arms around me, keeping me upright, and for the first time that day, I inhale. Closing my eyes, I trace the notes in his scent. Pinecones. Vanilla. And something woodsy.

"You can't keep me and expect a relationship, Dayton. I barely know you—"

"My soul knows you!" he snaps, peering into mine. "Please. Before you, I rarely begged for anything. Give me a chance, Sarah. You enjoyed it. You kissed me. Twice. That has to mean something." Desperation and loneliness carve his face.

He's mentally unwell, I remind myself, feeling my heart soften. He needs someone. A tear slips down my cheek. He stole me, hoping to have me find him someone. His brothers. More tears slip free. His brothers are just as traumatized and mentally unwell. He needs someone stable, someone... like me.

Am I honestly considering this? In nursing, I've learned that eyes rarely lie. It's why liars either avoid eye contact to decrease the risk of outing themselves or force it to lend credibility to their words. A seasoned bullshit sniffer sees through it all.

Pain. Madness. And raw grief shines in Dayton's eyes. There's no denying he's unstable, but he's also hurting, all alone in this fire-scorched house. I brought Lauren home, recognizing someone who needed me while I could provide.

Dayton's soul calls to mine in the same way, and I truly wish it didn't. If I leave and run away in the middle of the night, I suspect it'll haunt me as if I left my child behind. And I owe him for rescuing me from being assaulted.

"Ok, Dayton," I say around sniffles. "No more chains, no more drugs, and no more lies. Deal?" He nods, face filled with earnestness. Schizophrenic. In other words, a child in need of guidance. Poor impulse control. Poor emotional regulation. He needs someone to teach him all of it.

It hits me that I *cannot* let him eat my pussy again if I stay and help him. I'm definitely old enough to be his mother.

"No more touching," I tack on, watching a scowl crawl across his lips.

"No," he snaps, eyes shooting fire, fingers digging into my skin.

"Yes. It's wrong—"

"It does not feel wrong—"

"That's because you don't know right from wrong!" My shout rings in the empty space, and I wince. *Way to go, Sarah. Yell at the mentally unstable patient.*

"Dayton, I didn't mean to—"

"Fine. Call your daughter, then call my brothers." His hands release me, and I nearly stumble. His face shuts down, and the room feels colder for it. I feel like I kicked a puppy.

17

NO TOUCHING

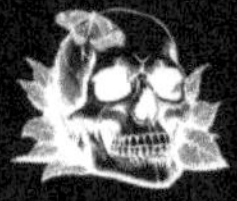

ZAIDEN

Honesty is not the best policy, and I want to kill whoever invented the phrase if someone hadn't beaten me to it. Sarah refused to step into the kitchen, forcing me to unravel the extra length of cord and hand it over at the threshold. She stared at me meaningfully, eyes suggesting I should trust her.

Grumbling, flanked by Blue and Red, I walk away, sitting on the bottom step a few feet away. She remains in my line of sight, but I'm far enough I can't overhear their conversation. But I catch her shooting frequent glances at me, turning away with a blush.

"No touching."

I detested the words the minute she uttered them. My mask remains in my hands, flipping from one to the other. She's seen my face and hasn't run, so there's no need to continue to hide, even if I want to.

"No touching."

What does that even mean? Twice, she gushed all over me. She kissed me, calming the chaos in my mind. *Why can't I touch?* It's a stupid rule, and I'm uncertain if I'll follow it.

Her feet pad over, and I'm on mine before she reaches me. A light pink adds color to her cheeks.

"Do you have a shower? One that won't fall beneath me?" My head tilts. Why would a shower fall?

My head jerks upstairs, and I open my mouth to offer to carry her, but she's shaking her head, staring at the pieces of the banister that crumbled. Oh, that's why she's worried about falling showers.

"I can carry you," I offer, shrugging my shoulders when really I want to throw her over them, slide her scrub bottoms off, and play with her wetness again, hearing her moans directly in my ear. My cock twitches, something it never did before her.

Down, boy.

"N-n-no, that's alright. How about you take me to my place—"

"No," I growl, prowling closer.

"Dayton—"

"You said you'd stay." My finger jabs at her, the threat implicit. She stays or else. No one will steal her from me. If I have to, I will slit my brothers' throat to prevent that. Xavier's woman had her mother long enough. She's mine now, touching or no touching.

She laughs unexpectedly, and I stumble back. It's new, cheeks pushed up into her eyes, narrowing them into squints, green sparks shining bright. I want to capture it so I can always remember it.

"You're being ridiculous. No more kidnapping, remember? We both can go to my place. How's that?" Her lips remain turned up in a smile, and the urge to kiss it off gnaws at me.

Me at Sarah's place? Just the two of us? My lips spread into a wicked grin, the edges nearly touching my ears. She flinches at witnessing my smile for the first time. I don't hide it. With Sarah, there will be no more hiding, and I'll remind her how good it felt with my mouth on her.

She'll let me touch, or I'll have to remove the hands of every male with eyes that cross her path. If I can't touch, neither can they.

SARAH

Holy shit, that smile is wicked creepy, a mimic of the Joker's, but seeing it in the flesh leaves me with pinpricks of dread. I never liked clowns.

Dayton remains oblivious or chooses to ignore my unease, reaching for my hand to entwine our fingers. I stare at them, roaming over the scars dotting the back of his hand. Armed with the knowledge of the disfigurement of his face, I'm certain he caused the scars on his hand, too.

Sighing, I let him lead me to the front door, reconciling I'm bringing a patient home essentially. Summoning anger over the events that transpired—the kidnapping, the nonconsensual oral—becomes futile. His excitement, the smile he shoots over his shoulder, infects me. It's contagious.

He's lonely. And I didn't miss him never answering me about his mom, but the grief lining his eyes suggests she died recently.

A hand tattooed with a macabre smile and circular eyes fists a key, inserting it into a deadbolt and springing the lock, opening the door to freedom. A warm breeze flies in, ruffling our hair. Sunlight brightens the eyes trained on me, matching the sky.

"No touching."

I can stick to that. Dayton leads the way, taking two careful steps over the threshold, neck swiveling back and forth in my direction as if reassuring himself I haven't disappeared.

Separation anxiety. Check.

I'm sure there are many others he's textbook for, but my fingers itch to look up his medical record now that I know his full name. Shame burns me at keeping his existence to myself. During my call with Lauren, I could tell Xavier drove while she and I spoke, undoubtedly with the Bluetooth on.

Lauren made idle chatter, recounting the events leading up to their trip. I expected anger but only found happiness in her voice. Xavier makes her happy, and I held my tongue about Zaiden's existence.

Why?

Unbidden, videos I've watched concerning re-homing pets flash behind my eyelids. They often take a week off, putting their pet on a schedule and letting them acclimate.

Dayton is not a pet!

But my subconscious hasn't shifted him out of the animal category. He behaves on instinct and lacks the morality to differentiate between right and wrong. Yet, excitement simmers low in my stomach, knowing I'm taking him home with me.

Like a damn new pet parent.

My feet brush grass, following the path Dayton leads to an aged, pale blue pickup truck. Wordlessly, I let him hold my waist, lifting me into the passenger side of his pickup truck. Once I'm seated, he remains standing near my spread thighs, gazing at me.

Before I have a chance to respond, he brushes a fleeting kiss over my lips, retreating with a smirk. My fingers brush my lips, watching him round the front of the truck to the driver's side. Swinging my legs in, I close the door after buckling my seatbelt.

Dayton doesn't make small talk, for which I'm grateful, the truck roaring to life with a wheeze. His hands draw my eyes, and I watch them with a handful of fascination, wrapping around the gearshift. He reverses the truck with quiet confidence, checking his rearview mirrors, long lashes fanning his cheeks.

My hands shoot to my mouth to ensure drool doesn't drip off the sides, helpless against the urge to watch him. He's a walking contradiction, I ruminate, watching trees flank us as he reverses out of a long, winding driveway. My mouth drops open when we reach the road, a wisp of fear embedded in my heart. The driveway was easily five miles long.

If I had escaped, would I have given up before reaching the road? His lips call to me, a small smile curling the long line of scars. He senses the direction of my thoughts but doesn't comment, driving in silence.

Sitting back in my seat, I admit to myself I never had a chance of getting away if I tried. And that's if I got the key to both deadbolts from him, the one to my cell and the front door.

I was completely at his mercy until whatever spurred him to sneak into my room and place his face between my thighs. A flush tints my face as I look out the window, refusing to look at him and give my thoughts away. I'd never admit defeat, but Dayton had truly gotten the best of me, keeping me contained.

The biggest question is, what happens now?

18

NOT ALONE

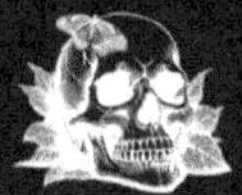

ZAIDEN

She doesn't speak on the drive, but I can feel her thoughts rampaging through that intelligent mind of hers. A glance in the rearview mirror reveals cars trailing behind us, and Red and Blue resting in the back seat. Tension tightens my shoulders. Sometimes, I wish I could leave my delusions behind, but they'd never let me be.

"She likes us," Red whispers to Blue, who grins wide, flashing even white teeth. *"She'll be ours. Just wait and see,"* the mellow doppelgänger whispers back.

My attention returns to the road, and I ignore all the signs.

Turn Back Now. There's No Escape. Hell is hot.

I shake my head, wishing the voices would quiet and quit pointing out billboards to me.

"Dayton, are you okay?" Sarah asks in a soft voice, a balm to the churning madness. My hand blindly reaches for her, and she doesn't hesitate to entwine our fingers, bringing my hand to rest against her chest. I dart a glance at her, and there's a softness to her expression, a muted under-standing, as if she knows what I'm thinking.

"It's hard, isn't it? Being in your head?" Swallowing hard, I nod, looking back at the road. We're close to her house, and I'm not far from a fucking breakdown. How can I keep her? Already my skin itches to peel itself off and crawl back to my mother's home.

"Talk to me then. Tell me about your mom." My heart doubles over in my chest, the organ wanting to defy biology and fall right out of me. *She wants to hear about my mom?*

"Zaiden," she whispers my name so quietly, barely above a whisper, but it unlocks something. Not bravery or courage but a desire to please her. It's all I ever wanted: to please my mom. Sarah reminds me of her so much now. Her gentle understanding, sweet voice, and touch don't make my skin rebel.

"She was sick." Tears cloud my eyes and clog my throat, but I push on for Sarah. "When she set the house on fire." I swallow down the memory wanting to drag me into the past, billows of smoke and screams taunting me. "The fire-fighters made it before the house burned down completely. They found me in her bed and took her away."

"I was asleep, but the smoke would've made sure I never woke up."

"Please! Zaiden! Please don't take my baby," my mother screams, soot and tears painting her face while men in uniforms drag her away. I try to run and follow, but an adult easily snatches me up, and I'm helpless to watch them take her from me.

"No one understood me. Soon, they said I was sick, too."

"Zaiden, when you think of your mother, how does it make you feel?" A man in a white coat asks, sitting across from me with a pad balanced on his knee. His eyes keep flicking to the scars on my hands. When the pain in my chest became too much, I split

my skin open. It quiets the voices, too. But I don't tell Mr. Impor-tant that, glaring him down in silence.

"They had me committed. When they released my mother, she visited every day, even hunting down my father to get them to expedite my release."

A stranger sits across from me, eyes a similar shade to my own. My lips twitch, cataloging the faint line of the wedding ring he removed, the bruised knuckles showing he got into a fight recently, and the faint whiff of alcohol coming off him.

Pathetic. That's what the voices say about him. We sit in silence until our visit is up, neither of us willing to break. I'll only speak to my mother, not the man who abandoned us for his other family. If I could burn my name from the history books and create a new identity, I would, just so Zaiden can stay buried.

"When I finally got out..." My teeth grind, fresh pain slicing through me.

"Cancer took her from me a second time." My fingers tighten around the steering wheel, destructive rage rising within me. "I miss her with everything I am." I can't say more, my throat closing up.

A hand brushes my lap, and I look down from the road at the placement. Sarah's hand rests just above my flaccid cock, and I snap my eyes to hers. Tears swim in green pools, and I know for certain they're for me.

"I'm sorry, and I know you've probably heard it a million times, and it changes nothing—"

"You've never said it," I interrupt. "When you say it, it changes something. It changes the fact that I'm not alone anymore." A horn blares, and I force my eyes back on the road. We're nearly at her house, and I can't wait to have her alone, minus the twins in the backseat.

Sarah makes me not feel alone anymore, and she's touching me. Surely, that means something?

SARAH

By the time we pull into my driveway, my emotions had muddied into slush. Dayton turns the truck off, sitting still with one hand on the gearshift, not looking at me. My instincts tell me he's waiting, waiting for another rejection, like he's received time and time again. So many people failed him.

I brush a hand across his cheeks, and his eyes close, face leaning into my touch. Other than his mother, had anyone touched him with affection? He appears starved for it. Turning his face, his eyes open to lock with mine. My heart seizes.

Complete adoration stares back at me, tugging on my heartstrings.

My lips tremble their way into a smile. In so many ways, he's childlike, calling on my motherly instincts. And in others, when my mind flashes back to his tongue between my legs, I'm reminded he's a grown man with a broken mind.

Slowly pulling away so he doesn't assume I'm rejecting him, I unbuckle my seatbelt, pull on the door, and jump down. Experience urges me to proceed with caution with Dayton. In my hands rests the power to destroy him or change his life for the better.

It'd be so much easier if he had been a child in my care. Glancing from my pink-painted front door, I shoot a look at Dayton, eyebrows raising.

"Do you have the key?" He flashes me another creepy smile. I don't think I'll ever adjust to his scars.

"I buried the spare in the backyard. Let me go fetch it,"

he says before jogging off, wild hair flopping around. He seriously needs a haircut.

I walk to the front door, running a palm down the paneled wood. I let Lauren paint it when she was eight. My forehead lands against the wood while I wrestle with my emotions.

"I've got it," Dayton rasps behind me. I nod, never changing positions, hearing him approach until his front grazes my back.

"Are you okay, Sarah?" A shudder travels down my spine, unconsciously arching against him. His hands land on my hips before moving up to cup my breasts, bringing his cock flush against my bottom.

"Are we still not touching?" he whispers, breath skating across my skin.

"Dayton," I gasp, resisting the urge to squirm against him. His cock jumps, and I cave, arching my back. He groans, bringing a hand to turn my head so his lips can ghost over mine.

"I want to touch, Sarah. With you, I want everything." My nipples harden, and I moan into his mouth, letting him claim me. His tongue slips into my mouth, collecting my taste. Moaning, I return the kiss, whimpering when his free hand brushes a hardened nipple.

Pulling his mouth back, eyes closed, swollen lips whisper, "Teach me, Sarah. Show me how to please you." I groan at his words, shifting forward.

He's so much like a child, and I feel dirty.

Thoughts flee when his hands slip beneath my shirt and calloused hands hold my breast.

"Dayton," I moan, leaning back against him.

"Don't do that, Sarah. Don't run from me. I know I'm different, but I want this, and you want this. Why push me away?" Confusion and a hint of anger flavor his voice.

Fuck. I'm messing this all up already.

"Dayton, we can't—" I don't get the words out, his hand slipping into the waistband of my pants and panties, aiming straight for my clit. My body bows, and a low moan slips from me, his deft fingers making circles.

"I want you to soak my hand like you did my face. I want your moans in my ear and your naked body in my arms," he growls in my ear, fingers picking up speed. My hand clamps over my mouth, hips rolling into his touch. He's going to make me come at my front door where anyone could see us.

"Dayton!" I shout when he pinches my clit, rubbing it between two fingers. My slick drips from me, coating his hand like he said. I nearly lose my mind when a thick digit prods my entrance. He shouldn't be doing this. I can't let him do this. Shaking my head, I open my mouth to say something, but only moans tumble out.

I'm coming. I'm so fucking coming, whimpering into the hot air, the sun beaming down on us. Dayton doesn't stop. Adding a second finger, breathing heavily in my ear.

"Give it to me, Sarah. Let go," he coaxes, and my eyes roll, body seizing as I do just that, coming on his fingers. His mouth slams into mine, tongue pushing in to re-stake his claim. My body goes limp, aftershocks lighting through me.

He doesn't remove his hand, thumb making slow circles, helping me ride it out. Pulling his mouth back, he shifts our weight, propping half of us against the door and unlocking the door with his free hand. He twists the door open, yanking me back like a limp doll so I don't fall forward.

My walls spasm around the fingers still in me, and I can't summon the energy to stop him. Liquid gushes from me when he finally removes his hand, and my eyes follow his hand to his mouth, his tongue licking the fingers clean.

He meets my stare, lips curling up. "Oh, that's just the

beginning, Sarah. I want inside, and you're going to let me. Aren't you?" he demands, bringing his face closer, and I nod weakly, my body still weak from the orgasm he wrenched from me.

Still smiling, he replies, "Good girl."

19
MINE

ZAIDEN

I cannot fucking wait to shove my cock inside of her. It's a throbbing ache in my pants, and I pick Sarah up in my arms, stepping over the threshold. She doesn't fight me, cheeks stained red. Good. All the better, she's not under the effects of drugs, allowing me to trust her body's reactions.

My feet kick the door closed, and I march up the stairs, aiming straight for Sarah's bedroom, throwing her on the bed as soon as I'm within touching distance. She bounces, staring at me wide-eyed. I turn to close her bedroom door, locking it for good measure. I'm claiming her, now!

Impatient fingers tug my shirt off, and I hear a gasp. I don't turn around, knowing she's tracking all of my scars. I couldn't care less about them. They're old and mostly made by my hand.

Kicking my boots off, my hands are tugging at my pants, shoving them down my legs until I'm standing naked in Sarah's bedroom. Turning, I watch her eyes lock on my hard cock. Her mouth drops open, but that won't do. She's still overdressed.

She can admire me later, after I've put my cock inside of her, emptying my seed into her pussy. I grin, knowing full well my woman isn't on birth control, patiently waiting for menopause to hit, but it hasn't yet, and I can already see her belly swelling with my child.

"Dayton, maybe we should talk—"

"No," I snap, scowling. "No more talking. More doing. Now, are you going to take your clothes off, or will I?" My hands gesture at her scrubs. She gives me a defiant look, eliciting pre-cum to bead on the tip of my cock. Oh, she's going to fight this. Good. I like her, both docile and feisty, the best of both worlds.

"Have it your way." That's the only warning she gets before I pounce on her. She twists and writhes beneath me, but I don't miss her dilated pupils, beaded nipples poking through her shirt. She wants this.

My hands pin her arms above her head, and she moans when I shove a hand back down her pants, hips rising off the bed.

"That's it," I croon, sliding a finger along her wet slit. With fascination, I watch the fight drain from her, hips lifting to meet my touch.

"These clothes are coming off. Do you understand?" She nods between moans. Such a good girl. She just needs reminding every now and then of how good I can make it. I wish she'd simply teach me instead of having to fumble my way through it, but I must be doing something right. I've made her body seize three times now.

Now, it's time to claim my girl.

SARAH

Pleasure tightens my nipples and wets Dayton's fingers between my thighs. I don't know what it is about his touch, but he brings me to the edge so easily it's criminal. I'm already coasting closer when he removes his hand and grips my waistband with both of his hands, yanking them down my thighs.

I lift my hips to help, and he tosses them to the floor before shoving up my shirt. I lean up and raise my arms, letting him remove my top and bra, laying back down, bared to him. He eyes me hungrily, taking all of me in. His tongue licks his lips, and I'm almost certain he's going to dive back between my legs, but he shakes his head as if dislodging the thought.

"I'm going to fuck you now, Sarah," he croaks, bringing a hand to stroke his hard length. My eyes follow the move-ment, staring at the tattoo above it. Snakes twist and twine above his cock with the head of two positioned on opposite sides, fangs bared like they're going to bite it off. *Who the fuck gets a tattoo like that?*

That train of thought gets interrupted when Dayton leans down, bracing both arms on either side of me. We stare into each other's eyes, blue to green.

"Spread your legs for me," he orders, eyes never leaving mine. I obey, fighting a whimper when he lowers his hips, cock teasing me.

"Dayton," I gasp, arching up. His smile is wicked. A hand comes up to cup my nape, and the other lifts my thigh higher, baring my pussy to him.

"Here we go, Sarah. It's you and me from here on out," he warns, tracing his lips over mine. I moan at the first brush of his cock against my opening.

"Yes, please, Dayton," I whimper, lifting my hips to help ease him inside of me. He shudders and thrusts forward, giving me an inch. My nails bite into his back. It feels so good. I need more.

"More, please." He nods, swallowing audibly, pushing more of his cock into me. I shove at his chest, and he hisses, releasing my thigh. I wrap both legs around his waist and he groans, sinking in all the way.

"Fuck, Sarah. That feels too good." His forehead rests on mine.

"Fuck me, Dayton," I moan, shifting beneath him. Eyes closed, he retreats, slamming back in, knocking the air from me.

"Yes," I cry out, tightening my entire body around him, keeping him close. When the fuck was the last time I had sex, or was it this good? If I did, I can't remember, losing myself in the rapid thrusts of Dayton's cock.

He takes his time with each retreat but makes hard thrusts inside of me. His eyes remain closed, savoring our connection, and if I had doubts about his virginity, the pure bliss on his face erases them.

My nails drag down to his taut ass, and I dig in, forcing him to fuck me harder. Hissing, he loses restraint, hips slamming into me until my walls are fluttering around his thick cock. His bare chest brushes my nipples on each glide, and I'm shoved over the edge, screaming his name, pussy clenching around his cock.

"Sarah!" he shouts, thrusts stuttering before I feel his cock jerking inside me, spilling his seed. Fuck. We didn't use protection, but he doesn't stop dragging his cock in and out of me, hardening with each thrust and retreat.

Oh shit. He's going to fuck me into oblivion. My arms wrap around his neck, holding on for the ride, feeling myself crest toward another climax.

"That's it, Sarah," his lips kiss my neck. "Take all of me. Let me give it to you. You're mine now." One of his hands wraps around my throat, choking me. "This pussy," he says, retreating, hips slamming forward. "Is. Mine." A thrust punctuates the words.

I come around his cock again with a choked moan, eyes rolling back. Dayton is fucking wrecking me, and I let him, going limp beneath him as he keeps giving me his cock, over and over again.

20

GOODBYE

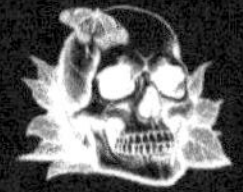

SARAH

Warm skin rests beneath my cheek, rising and falling, pushing my head up and down. My lips curl into a silly smile. Goosebumps rise beneath my fingers, tracing random swirls into the raised skin. Scars line nearly every inch of Dayton's body, spelling a sad tale, one I've witnessed over and over during my stint in the emergency room.

My heart squeezes for him, imagining his life before me, the loneliness that dogged him in those facilities that treated him like an insect. His chin slides against my nose as I turn my face up, finding his eyes already trained on me. Scars stretch, and white teeth gleam in the light. Happiness dances in aqua eyes, a warm pool rippling to reflect the sunlight.

"What are you thinking, my Sarah?" he whispers, gravel voice slipping across my senses like a physical touch. I'm thinking I'm in over my head. I don't say that, tracing the edge of one facial scar, muscles jumping beneath my touch.

"You did all of these. Will you tell me why?" I ask. Dark lashes rest on high cheekbones, shutters shielding his eyes from me.

"Because it quieted the voices. Until it didn't," he croaks, voice sounding raw and raspy. My hand stills. Voices. Schizophrenia. I allow my own eyes to close, shutting down the initial bias and fear. Blood in the ceiling. I already know what he's capable of, and aside from kidnapping me, I'm unharmed. No, my body is loose and sated, lying across his naked form.

"You're scared?" he asks. My eyes pop open, tracking the wariness glinting in his cerulean pools. I brush a kiss across his lips, feeling his groan travel to my sore sex.

"No. I'm checking my own prejudice," I tell him, fingers still stroking his face. "Too many times we have these knee-jerk reactions, but they mask how we really feel if we don't look closer. I'm not afraid, Dayton. Cautious? Yes. But not afraid of you." Sincerity layer my words. He worries me, and stress attacks me with all the possibilities of how this could go wrong, but fear isn't my knee-jerk reaction.

"Do you hear voices now?" I cringe at my question, remembering all the times I asked that during clinicals. It's a standard assessment question on several forms. He shakes his head, dark hair brushing his forehead. My hand pushes it back, reveling in the softness of his hair and the warmth of his skin.

My teeth worry my lip at my next question. Dayton bravely lifts a hand, pulling the lip free, eyes beseeching me for honesty and openness like a child would. His innocence and childlike behavior, at times, squeeze my heart even tighter. I'm weak to it. For the first time, I wonder if he's not still holding me captive, using emotional tethers instead of physical ones.

"Would you consider getting medicated?" My teeth

nibble at my lip again, eyes bouncing everywhere to avoid looking at his initial reaction. Even to my ears, the question sounded brass.

"I'd do it for you," he confesses, lips rubbing along the seam of mine. "I'd do a lot for you, Sarah." His admission tightens my nipples, wetness flooding my core. It wouldn't surprise me if wetness dripped down my thighs, landing on one of his legs from my thigh strung across his lower body.

What has he done to me?

I worked hard for my doctorate in nursing, turning a blind eye to those who insist on calling me Nurse Bell instead of Dr. Bell. I'm not some weak creature to fall for a guy after a few orgasms, but something about Dayton tugs on my heartstrings, luring me to lower my walls, to take a second look beyond the scars and kidnapping.

A lonely kindred spirit lurks in his eyes, whispering a siren song.

"Dayton," I whisper, need curling in my stomach with greedy fingers. Lips brush mine, tongue sweeping in, an answer poised on his tongue.

Mine. Each stroke, each brush, screams *mine.* I don't fight it, letting my walls down, sinking into the feeling of being just Sarah, not Dr. Bell or Mom. To Dayton, I am merely Sarah. I've never felt more free, allowing him to roll me onto my back, legs spread to allow him to settle between them.

Mine, my mouth answers his claim, staking one of my own. He's mine, my captor, my lover. My nails scrape along his scalp, legs winding around his waist. When his cock sinks into me, I'm lost, swept away by the pleasure only he brings to my body.

He claims me with each thrust of his hips, nails digging into my skin. My hips rise to meet him each time, clamping down around his cock, claiming him every time my walls pulse, pulling him deeper.

Dayton is *mine.* His name leaves my lips on a weak cry, body tightening. Slumping into the mattress, letting him pound into me to claim his own release, I've never felt more free.

Being claimed by Dayton makes my heart sing a song of freedom, limbs going lax.

ZAIDEN

Soft hair tickles my chin, and light snores escape Sarah's mouth, bringing a smile to mine. I twirl strands of thick hair around my forefinger, waiting for sleep to claim me as it did Sarah, her warm body resting on my chest.

Contentment, the first I've ever experienced, settles in my bones. My limbs feel lax, a soft euphoria running through me. I lost count of how many times Sarah screamed my name, sweet pussy clenching around me, wringing every drop of seed until I felt like she drained my soul. Such pleasure was also a novelty.

I'm eager to do it again and again, but her drowsy eyes, gazing up at me, compelled me to let her rest, or I'd rut her all night. The sun fell not long ago, shadows creeping into the bedroom. Quick feet running across carpet has me bolting upright, cradling Sarah. She mumbles, but I hush her, recognizing a pair of blue eyes gazing at me from the foot of the bed.

Little Brother. Another apparition of my mind. He hefts himself into the bed, crawling toward me and Sarah. I lie back down, my precious treasure tucked close. She resumes snoring.

Little Brother rests his head on a pillow near mine, and the two of us gaze up at the ceiling. Sliding a glance at him, I gape, noting the burns on his face disappeared. *When and why did that happen?*

"*I like her,*" he whispers, voice pitched low. Red and Blue are absent.

"*What happened to your face?*" I ask him, running my eyes over the rest of his small body, sporting a set of fire truck pajamas. He appears as the same age I was when they took my mother, but the flames that night never touched me. Or did they?

He returns my stare, shifting into a fetal position. His lips lack the scars mine have.

"*It's time to let me go,*" he says, and I shake my head. Together, we ran through our mother's house, playing tag, hiding in places we shouldn't, and pulling pranks that drove our mother mad. Why would he leave me now?

His wise eyes land on Sarah, then shift back to me. I clutch her tighter, hating the understanding sprawling into my mind. An only child living in the creepy Daniels' Manor with no friends, no playmates, and a mother who talked to apparitions of her own. Little Brother played with me, sharing secrets and nightmares, huddling close during storms.

But he's as real as Red and Blue. I blink rapidly, tears collecting on my lashes, fingers digging into Sarah's bare skin. *Is this the price for her? Losing the only friends my mind could conjure up?*

A small hand lands on my shoulder, and he gives me a sad smile before brushing a phantom kiss across Sarah's hair. A blink and he's gone. It's just me and Sarah, as I promised it would be when I put my cock inside of her.

Silence presses in, all-encompassing and mocking. It is taunting, trying to tease out whispers. My mind remains eerily silent, a fresh grave waiting for a corpse to fall in. Sarah rests on my chest, sleeping peacefully, oblivious to the chaos lashing beneath my skin.

"It's this house. The walls, the voices, all of it. Do you hear them, baby?" My mother kneels before me, clutching my shoulders in a bruising grip. Brown eyes bounce around in every direction, only occasionally locking on my eyes before flicking away like someone beyond me pulls her attention away. But we're alone.

I rock to the left, rolling until Sarah lies beneath me, black hair spread out across the pillows, looking like spilled ink. Trailing a finger across a cheek, I lean to brush an airy kiss across her parted lips, face lax in slumber.

"I'll be back," I whisper, skin prickling, ghosts tugging at me, luring me back to Daniels' Manor.

"I'll finish what she started, then I'll be back. Wait for me, little raven." I brush errant strands off her forehead, heart twisting in my chest. Only my mother used to make it flip and somersault until Sarah pumped new life into my lifeless body. I cannot begin anew with my raven until I've burned the past to ashes and cinders, burying my misdeeds with them, mind flickering to the severed limbs in my fridge.

Little Brother has left me, but Red and Blue will return, along with the voices of the others.

Purge. That's the term my mind locks on. I need to purge the illness from me, to be better for Sarah. Nodding to myself, I ease out of the bed, bending down to retrieve discarded clothing.

Making it to the door, I afford myself one final look at the temptress in the bed, tangled sheets wrapped around her lush form.

"I'll be back," I mouth again, turning my back on my redemption.

Once more, I'll walk from the flames burning Daniels' Manor, stepping into a new dawn with Sarah and the half-brothers she'll introduce me to. I'll accept nothing less.

21

DISAPPEARED

SARAH

Blinking open my eyes, my heart sinks at the empty bed cocooning my lax body. Sitting upright, I glance around my bedroom, devoid of Dayton's tall, muscular frame. My tongue swipes across my lips furiously, mind swimming with possibilities.

He left?

Swinging myself out of bed, sheet clutched to my naked body, I pad to my bedroom door, pulling it open.

"Dayton!" I call down the hall, listening for a reply. Walking out of my bedroom, down the hall and stairs does nothing to erase the confusion swamping me. Dayton's gone. My empty house mocks me, cream walls taunting me with their barrenness. Barren, like me.

Feeling numb, I sink to the bottom step of my stairs, staring at my feet. My face falls into my waiting hands, elbows digging into my thighs. The sheet pools around me, cool air kissing my skin.

I can't believe he left. Without a word. Shoving my hair back, I'm fighting tears as I race back up the stairs, a small kernel of hope burying itself into my chest. When my hands snatch up my phone, trembling fingers nearly misdial.

One ring. Two—

"Hey, Mom. We're nearly there. Are you okay? You sounded weird the other day," Lauren says, picking up mid-ring. My eyes close, remembering our last call occurred before I let my guard down with Dayton, sharing my body and sliver of my heart with him.

"I'm fine, baby. Have you heard from Zaine? I was just checking if he's had any strange visitors. I got this feeling of being followed last week." I swallow the lump in my throat, hand pressed to my forehead. Dayton was the presence stalking me, inciting my night terrors.

"No, not that we heard of. Right, Xavier?" He mumbles something in the background, and I resist rolling my eyes. No amount of time will dull my rage at him for stealing my baby.

"Nope. Did you call the police or ask Auntie Nat to sleep over?" Lauren asks. Wind whooshes across the line. I can only assume they're still driving, taking back roads to their destination.

"Nat was here for a little while last week," I admit, nibbling my lip. I'm out of options. I've no idea where he went, and fresh pain blooms beneath my ribs.

"Be safe. I love you. I'll talk to you later," I say, quickly ending the call and slumping into my bed. Tears stream down my face. Once more, I bury my face in my hands, letting the sobs leave me. He left. God, I can't even maintain a relationship with a damn kidnapper.

Self-deprecation sinks its claws into me. I try to shake it off, wiping at my cheek with unsteady hands. This isn't me. I let him get in my head, manipulate me, falling for the poor mental patient act. I should know better. Air wheezes in and out of my lungs rapidly, tingling traveling up from my fingers.

I rush to my dresser, snatching open the drawer where I keep spare bottles of Ativan. Fumbling with the first bottle I grab—pop.

"Fuck!" I scream, sinking to my knees, crying as I pick up fallen pills. The tears won't stop. Fucking Lasher. They're nothing but trouble. My back thuds against my dresser, knees tucked into my chest.

I wrap my arms around my tucked legs, laying my face on the top of my knees. Shaking my head, I can't stop berating myself for my moments of weakness. The only thing I can ask myself, sitting naked in my lonely bedroom, discarded pills winking at me, is what now?

ZAIDEN

Ghosts haunt Daniels' Manor, my ancestors strolling across the overgrown lawn. Gravel crunches beneath the tires of my pickup truck, a truck passed from my grandfather to my mother to me. It wheezes upon every startup but faithfully transports me to where I need to go.

I park the relic where it belongs, directly in front of the decrepit door of my childhood home, vines crawling over the chipped wood. In. Out. I force myself to breathe, to not trust anything my eyes see. Already, I ache for Sarah, for her calm reassurance and gentle understanding. She may not know the chaos of my mind, but she knows how to navigate it—to lead me back to the light.

Stiff limbs push the truck driver's door open, stepping down with dread, eyes focused on my boots, rustling coming closer. I slam the door shut, marching through the overgrown weeds to the front door, echoes sounding loud as gunshots. Quick feet race all around me, but I ignore them.

Voices clamor for space in my head. I race through the manor, a gossamer gown clinging to my body. Zaiden sleeps upstairs, but I'll make the world safer for him. I'll burn this place down, ripping this evil from the world. The devil whispers to me in my sleep, and I hear him talking to Zaiden. I must protect my child, hands wrapping around a red gallon of gasoline. It's the only way.

The front door creaks open, wood shifts beneath my weight, and I march toward the kitchen. A gallon of gasoline rests underneath a cabinet. Screams roll through the manor, many voices lifting into one. Either the house or the voices know what I'm attempting, nearly bringing me to my knees.

Zaiden! I internally scream, clamping my hands over my ears. Screams resound through the house, bouncing off the walls. The house, the voices dislike my actions, urging me to switch paths. But my dark-haired child with shadows in his eyes needs me. He needs me to slay the demons around us. I will do it for him. My mouth opens, an echoing scream ripping free, taunting the madness swimming in my head. It will have to kill me before I abandon my mission, abandon Zaiden.

My beacon, my anchor, the safe harbor I strive to reach, flashes in my mind, cheeks lifted and eyes squinted into a brilliant smile. I will find my way back. Devils be damned.

I scream back at the house, hands tearing at my hair, chest hollowing out. This is my home! I lived here, a part of me died here, and my sanity was ripped from me here. Daniels' Manor will not claim me as its victim. It will bow beneath me, or I will rip it limb from limb like any animal I'd ever caught.

Tears drip down my cheeks, hands shaking liquid free from the nozzle of the bottle I hold with both hands. An acrid stench tickles my nose, but I continue my work, heart aching to hold Zaiden in my arms. One more pass through the house then I can hold him, kissing his forehead and promising him the world is a safe place. I will make it so. Trust me, my dear child.

My hands close around a red gallon, déjà vu settling beneath my skin, a mocking presence tempting my brain to stop and turn back. Danger lurks here. I am the last of the Daniels, a mad bloodline's walking death, but Sarah's voice in my ear, asking me about my mother, Morgan, pushes back against the devil.

I am hers.

I will end this for her or die in the process. Either way, I've found my angel and will wait for her forever if I need to.

Once I douse the first floor, spilling extra in the kitchen, I gird myself for the trip into the basement. My boots stomp through the debris, carving a path to the door leading to my mother's tomb. It swings open easily, darkness staring at me below the set of stairs. My boots thump down them, the noise in my head picking up and growing in volume with each step.

A small pull on a flimsy bit of string chases the shadows away, light flooding the room. My mother rests in a glass enclosure, eyes forever closed, dark hair trailing to her hips, and a white dress—one of her favorites—adorns her stiff corpse. My hand lands on the glass, tears stinging my eyes.

"Goodbye, Mom. I've found someone," I confess, lips twitching into a smile. "I think you'd like her. She's a doctor. A nurse doctor. She understands my mind on some level. I hope you're happy wherever you are." I lean down, placing a watery kiss on the glass, tears dripping down my cheeks.

How do people do this and just move on, letting go? My heart aches, a giant pain I have trouble breathing around, knowing I must finish what she started. After tonight, I'm never setting foot back in Daniels' Manor, burning my mother's body, pieces of Sarah's coworkers, and the rest of the decrepit building to the ground.

"You're really doing this?" Red growls behind me. I don't turn, feeling rage waft off of him.

"It needs doing," I grit out, closing my eyes, wishing the voices away.

He's not real. He's not real. He's not real. He's not real.

"Enjoy her," Blue says, boots crunching closer. *"But when she discards you, we'll always be here,"* he promises, hand landing on my shoulder. I look at him, at his hand tapping against his skull. Blue commanded my mouth in the institute, charming the nurses and helping me pretend to be normal. He's the version of myself I wish I could be all the time, a mask I don to hide my insanity.

Red grips my other shoulder, fingers digging in, pain tethering us. Red manipulated my body, using it to defend us, to shield me from pain, absorbing all of it and turning it into rage. Nostrils flaring, he nods his head, giving his approval, stepping back, and locking eyes with Blue.

I close my eyes, refusing to witness them disappear and leave me like Little Brother. A snap, heard only by me, ricochets in my head and I know they're gone.

It's time to end this.

I'm coming back, little raven.

22

A WEEK LATER

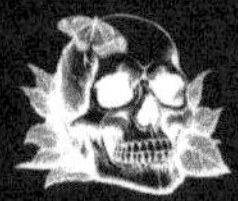

SARAH

A heaviness rests on my heart. I ignore it, adjusting the pillows behind Ms. Delores, a smile not reaching my eyes, promising to check back on her in a few minutes. She nods gratefully, a silent dismissal.

Stepping out of her room, my hand snakes to my sternum, pressing on the ache resting behind it. A week. A week and no word from Dayton or the five coworkers that went on leave, never returning on the date they gave human resources. Travel nurses run rampant through my unit like little cockroaches. And maybe it's my imagination, but whispers follow me every time I exit a room.

Circles rest beneath my eyes. I shrug off the lack of sleep. It pales to the sleepless nights spent at Lauren's bed whenever she got sick. She's not of my blood, but she definitely inherited my stubborn streak.

I nod to Cynthia, the charge nurse, blindly walking to my next patient's room, non-slip shoes squeaking over the linoleum floors, antiseptic scenting the air. A quick check at the clock adorning the wall reveals an hour is all that remains of my shift. It can't come soon enough, and I pray none of my patients go into labor, energy reserves too depleted to focus on bringing a new life into this world.

Dayton. I don't allow my mind to dwell on him long, bitterness and heartache soaring every time his name pops into my head. He took what he wanted and disappeared. End of story.

Ms. Cynthia smiles brightly at me when I enter her room after knocking, hands resting on her rounded belly. At thirty-eight weeks, her skin glows, and a peculiar light shines in her brown eyes.

"How are you feeling, Ms. Cynthia?" I ask, eyes cataloging her tells. A steady pulse throbs in her neck, with no spike indicating distress. The machines beat steadily without alarm. I'm moving to her side, sliding a hand to manually check her pulse before she answers.

"Oh, I'm feeling good. I'm starting to think Paul and I were being paranoid coming in for a little cramping," she replies blithely, inhaling deeply. I frown, watching her chest rise and fall, counting her respirations. My lips move without my knowledge, keeping her talking, but my eyes remain focused on her chest, years of experience honing in on an innocuous sign.

Shit. Twelve breaths per minute. She keeps talking, oblivious to the amount of work her lungs are performing to keep pumping air into her and her baby. My face remains jovial, smile fixed in place, and I promise to return after confirming the machine has an accurate heart rate. One hundred beats per minute.

Retreating, I ignore the grumble in my stomach, a reminder I skipped breakfast and ate a bag of chips in between five patients. Whether she knows it or not, Ms. Cynthia isn't far from entering premature labor.

It's going to be another long night, and I beeline for the breakroom's coffee machine. I'll call Dr. Scott after I am caffeinated. Delivering a child without caffeine for blood is asking for trouble.

ZAIDEN

A WEEK AGO

Knock. Knock. Knock.

"Alright, I'm coming! Hold your horses," a gruff voice calls through the thin piece of wood posing as a door.

"Kick it down."

"Break in and kill him."

"She'll never love you."

My eyes shut, molars grinding against each other. It took everything within me not to go straight to Sarah as soon as flames licked the insides of Daniels' Manor. After leaving the basement, I'd performed one final farewell before setting a match to the place.

Sheba. I set her free near the woods farthest from the manor, running back to finally finish what my mother and I started.

Staring into the dancing flames, saying farewell to my mother and imaginary companions, I couldn't ignore the other apparitions stalking the grounds and voices loitering in my head.

I no longer know what's real and what isn't, trees blurring into shadows stretching toward me with spindly limbs. Showing up at Sarah's door, smoke and ash staining the same clothing I've worn for three days, isn't an option.

"Know when to ask for help," Dr. Shaw used to say. His eyes always lanced me, seeking the root of my problems. The door cracks open. A narrowed green eye looks me up and down.

"You look like shit, my boy," Dr. Shaw remarks, not opening the door further.

"I need help," I confess, sinking to my knees. Twenty-four hours. It took twenty-four hours for the house to burn, roof caving in and burying my sins. I'd read once that the mind can't function well during sleep deprivation. Mine rarely functions when I am sleeping.

A slippered foot enters my vision before the rest of the kneeling older man does. Weathered hands land on my shoulders, and a clinical gaze runs over me. I let him, accustomed to the same unspoken assessment from the facilities. Even my Sarah did it, unaware that I could see her mind working through my symptoms.

Finally, he nods after a moment, groaning as he stands and motions me up.

"Come on in," he says, walking ahead of me. I follow him inside, sliding the locks into place.

"By the way, I'm retired. So, you better find a hell of a way to make this up to me. I've got a guest room you can sleep in and maybe some old clothes you can squeeze into," the old man says, moving further into the house.

Shock immobilizes my limbs. He let me in. He's offering help. Blood stains my hands, and I'm not sure if it's real or imagined.

"Dr. Shaw," I whisper, tears clinging to my lashes. He pokes his head around the corner, white hair sticking up. A sly smile curls his lips, reminding me of my time as his patient. He taught me the meaning of the term "as clever as a fox." He hadn't changed, capable of talking me into the most complex circles. I'd never met another mind like his, except for maybe my raven.

Fingernails bite into my palms. I'm doing this for her.

Dr. Shaw's shoulder leans against the frame of the doorway he'd entered.

"Everyone needs help at some point, Zaiden." A faraway look enters his eyes, staring unseeing past a point beyond my head.

"People forget to treat the person instead of the illness, forgetting that patients are people at the end of the day. I imagine that if someone other than myself took that approach, your treatment might have reaped more success."

Emerald pools shift and ripple with a multitude of emotions, and I'm no longer certain Dr. Shaw is looking at me or past patients he'd failed to save.

"Take the olive branch, Zaiden, and get help. Real help this time. You don't have to walk this road alone." His stooped frame straightens. "And I'm sorry about your mother. I saw the news report about a fire at your child-hood home." His gaze locks meaningfully on the soot deco-rating my clothing, showcasing my guilt.

A white brow cocks. "I don't have to worry about my golden years going up in a puff of smoke, do I?" I bark a choked laugh, shaking my head. My mother's ghost lands a hand on my shoulder, also silently urging me to trust Dr. Shaw, to take his offer of help. I wasn't sure I was chasing a dream or an apparition through the streets, screaming her name, until I came upon a car I recognized.

Through barred windows with eyes heavily lidded from drugs, I used to watch Dr. Shaw scramble into the beat-up green Toyota. I'd recognize his car anywhere. Sarah's smile flashes in my mind, along with flickering images of her body writhing beneath me.

I want that again. I want her, and I can't have her as I am, unmedicated and unable to discern what's real.

My head nods before I give the command, errant tears

streaking down my face. For my raven, I'd burn the damn world to ruins, spelling out her name in the ashes, whistling over the crackle of buildings collapsing.

"For Sarah," I whisper in a voice too soft for Dr. Shaw to hear, shuffling closer so he could show me to the guest bedroom.

23

LITTLE RAVEN

ZAIDEN

A **Week Later**

My fist connects with the cushioned glove sheathing Dr. Benji Shaw's hands. A left jab strikes the right glove. Another hook hits the other glove, the sound of the impact bouncing off the walls of the basement. I extend my arm again, putting force behind the punch. And again. And again. Unsatisfied, blood rushing to my head, I raise my leg impulsively, striking out. The top of my foot collides with the glove, sending Dr. Shaw flying off his feet, breath whooshing out of him.

Panting, forcing my breathing to slow, I battle with the guilt swirling through my dilated veins. My feet slap the mats decorating the concrete floor, striding to help Dr. Shaw to his feet. Parting my lips to apologize, a liver-spotted hand waves me off.

"This is why we have mats," Benji wheezes, one hand pressing to his lower back. Shit. *Can I do nothing right?*

"How do you feel?" he asks me, shrewd eyes narrowing

slightly. Raking a hand through my hair, I close my eyes, slowing my breathing as he taught me.

"We are here."

"Go to her."

"Angry," I answer honestly, eyelids popping open. He nods, walking toward one of the couches pushed against the cement walls. His butt sinks into the stiff cushions, dust floating up into the air, irritating our noses. He waves a hand, coughing slightly.

"Anger is good. Feeling something is better than not feeling anything, or—" he cocks a brow, "pretending not to feel anything. Now, tell me honestly. This is all for a woman?" His eyes see too much. They always did. Angling my body away from him, throat swallowing several times, I nod.

She is unhappy, dark circles shadowing emerald eyes. Dr. Baker insists it takes four to six weeks to see results from the new medication he's started me on. Until then, I watch my raven from the shadows, witnessing her returning home later and, later, working longer shifts each day. It's a slow death, watching the light drain out of her.

"She's everything," I whisper, lips barely moving. Already two interviews laughed me out the door, only allowing me entry as a favor to Dr. Shaw. Each time, blood would fall from the sky, staining my hair, skin, and clothing. Returning to my guest bedroom in Dr. Shaw's home, I'd watch the walls shift, breathing in and out, hands stretching for me through the aged wallpaper.

"The medicine can't fix me," I tell him, fear clutching my chest. It's a fear I've avoided voicing until now.

"It's not supposed to," he says. My head snaps to him, eyebrows rising to my hairline.

"Because there's nothing to fix, Zaiden. You're not broken, just different." Groaning, he pushes himself to his feet, locking eyes with me, young to old.

"Let's go again. And this time, tell me the name of every doctor or healthcare professional that's failed you. Purge them from your mind, Zaiden. You'll be better for it and," his hand gestures beyond the walls, "so will that woman of yours. Come on. Hit me again."

He shuffles to the middle of the room, and I dutifully follow him, a duckling following in the steps of its elder.

"We can do one more round before your interview at Mercy Hospital. This one will hire you. I'm sure of it. They need strapping young men to clean floors."

Barking a laugh and feeling everything but young or strapping, I shift into a defensive stance with Dr. Barker's name teasing the edge of my tongue.

SARAH

Creamy liquid mocha swirls in the black coffee, promising sweetness. It didn't deliver on cup one or two, but I stir the straw for cup three with false optimism. Ms. Cynthia started contractions an hour after I contacted Dr. Scott. Baby hasn't arrived by hour four, and I'm doubling down on caffeine for the long haul.

Bringing the cup to my lips, I hear footsteps before a throat clears.

"I'm on Dr. Scott's team. If you need help to lift a patient, can you grab someone else? I need to be free in case Ms. Cynthia is ready to push." Exhaustion and a mild dose of irritation taint my voice, but I'm too tired to care, running on fumes. Keeping my back to the newcomer, I take my first sip of mediocre coffee. It goes down like sludge, causing an all-body shudder.

"I'm actually looking for you, Sarah," a familiar voice rasps behind me. My heart seizes, and I whirl around, nearly spilling my coffee.

Dayton's lips curl up in a nervous smile. With flowers clutched in his hands, he shuffles in the doorway when I don't immediately respond. My mouth can't make words; too dumbfounded to see him in my workplace.

He prowls closer, keeping the flowers in front of him like a shield. I run my eyes all over him, heart squeezing tighter at the dated suit hugging his muscular frame and the haircut he didn't have a week ago. He'd cut it short and shaved the sides, with a long fringe in the front sweeping his forehead.

Tears blur my vision. I actually love the damn haircut. Lips trembling, my free hand comes to my mouth, holding back sobs. How dare he!

"I'm sorry for leaving, little raven," he starts, gesturing the flowers at me. I don't take them, waiting to hear more. He swallows. "I had to take care of something." His voice dips into a whisper. "I burned the house," he admits.

"My coworkers?" A tendril of fear skates through me. He nods, lids lowering to shield his eyes.

"I won't do it again. Not unless someone hurts you or you're pregnant and need—" I launch myself at him, clutching my cup of coffee between us, inhaling deeply of his scent, and letting my tears fall freely.

His arms wrap around me, the bundle of flowers pressing into my back.

"I missed you, but I needed to get better, to be better. You deserve better." I shake my head against his neck. I'd never asked him to change, even though the clinician in me knew he needed psychiatric help, more than I could provide.

He pulls back, and I'm tempted to cling to him, but let him gently push me back so he can look into my eyes.

"I did a job interview here a few hours ago for an environmental service position. They hired me on the spot, and I wanted to surprise you." My lips drop open, forming an O. *He got a job?*

"I also had an appointment earlier in the week and got prescribed antipsychotics." He gives me a wary look, waiting for my reaction. I have none, silent tears streaking down my face. All of this. It's so much more than I expected.

He continues, "I can't promise I'll keep taking them or worry they'll make me feel less like me, but—" I turn my back, place my cup of coffee down, and throw myself back at this sweet, sweet man.

His mouth crashes into mine, our tongues meeting like long-lost friends. Him. I want him. I pull away to say just that.

"I'm much too old for you—"

"You're fucking perfect, Sarah," he growls against my mouth, dampening my panties.

"But," I continue, laughing at his interruption. "I want this. I want you." His forehead rubs up and down mine with the nodding of his head.

"Me, too."

Our eyes remain locked, and we stand there, staring into the other, letting our hearts and breaths become in sync. In that moment, nothing else mattered.

24

I'M HIS

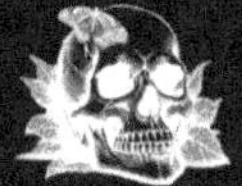

ZAIDEN

A soft drizzle of rain patters my head. I ignore it, watching auras weave and bleed around the oblivious pedestrians striding in and out of the hospital. It's like a never-ending stream of people. Time ceases meaning anything to me, pupils jumping from one aura to another, lips twitching at the color array.

"Dayton?" My head snaps toward the voice, feeling it creep into my cerebrum, stroking the folds of my brain.

"Sarah," I whisper, euphoria bursting inside of me. Stiff limbs rise from their seated position outside of the emergency room exit. Wide green eyes roam over me.

"You're soaked. How long have you been out here?" she asks, hurrying toward me. My scars stretch wide, flashing a toothy grin at the center of my universe. I'd wait forever for her. She wants me. She said so, however, long ago. Running feet had interrupted our interlude, and she promised to seek me out at the end of her shift before racing out of the room to join the running feet.

I thought I'd save her the trouble and wait for her

outside of the hospital, letting the mirage of colors distract me from my scattered thoughts.

"Come on," she says, waving her hand to the side. "Let's get you inside my car before it rains even harder." Her arm loops through mine, leading forward. I go willingly. After all, I'm hers.

"Are you sure you're okay?" Sarah asks again, concern brightening her eyes. It's sweet. Only my mother used to worry about me. My head nods again, tired eyes blinking furiously to stay open. She laughs, unbuckling her seatbelt before exiting the car.

I follow, grimacing at my wet clothing skating across her leather seats. She assured me it was fine, but fear kept surging in my veins, whispering that she'd change her mind and put me out on the side of the road. It hasn't happened, and we've arrived at her home, feet carrying me toward the pink-painted door. Sarah shoots me a coy smile, unlocking the door and holding it open for me.

For some odd reason, my heart seizes, temporarily halting blood flow, flooded with apprehension. Is this real? What if it's all a delusion, a vivid fever dream?

Maybe my Sarah knows more than me, abandoning her position at the door to close the distance between us, slender fingers lacing with my numb ones. I can't even speak, tongue lying useless in my mouth. A light tug forces my unreliable legs to walk forward until I'm crossing the threshold, listening to the click of the door closing and Sarah engaging the locks.

What now? I wonder, air wheezing out of my dry mouth. I want her, and she wants me. It doesn't eliminate the fear that I'll screw it all up, watching flames burn our burgeoning relationship to ash. I burned my childhood home. Nothing says I won't burn this before flowers can bloom from our fledgling stalk.

Footsteps slide across the floor, coiling the tension in me tighter. My eyes track Sarah, neck turning to watch her walk from the door at my back to stand in front of me, lips curling upwards. What does she have planned? My cock jumps in my pants, eager to find out, to serve her in any way I can.

SARAH

He's nervous. Scared. Tension lines his entire body, eyes darting around the room, never meeting mine. Why does that tighten my nipples and send heat flooding my sex, damp panties sticking to me? I'm still in disbelief that he sat outside my job for over three hours, rain pelting his hair and clothes.

But he's all mine.

I point a finger at his chest, cocking a brow, secretly wondering if he'll obey.

"Strip." The command leaves my lips as a soft and breathy sound, filling up the space of my living room. I've missed him, missed how he filled me, missed the obsession shining in his eyes. I'm a forty-three-year-old nurse. I've delivered more babies than attended dates this year.

None of that matters when Dayton claims me. To him, I'm merely Sarah. How many men have looked at me with an ounce of the depth of infatuation that deepens Dayton's gaze? None.

His hands hurriedly fly up to his chest, unbuttoning buttons in a mad rush. Redness races across his neck and cheeks, but he doesn't stop undressing, tossing his jacket, shirt, and pants carelessly to the floor. He's eager to please me, and the knowledge is addictive and heady. I alone wield this power over this impressive specimen, muscles bunching and scars reflecting the light.

My mouth waters, soft pants leaving me as he removes his boxers, the last stitch of clothing shielding him from my gaze. He's not coy or shy, standing in front of me, hands held loosely at his side. No, hunger burns in his eyes, but he stands still for my inspection, eagerly awaiting my next order.

It shouldn't arouse me. I shouldn't get involved with my kidnapper and stalker, but Z claimed me from that first kiss. He owns me. I was just oblivious to it until his cock filled me, despair assailing me when I discovered his departure the morning after. He's done all of this for me, being such a good boy.

I am his, and he is mine. My fingers crook at him, beckoning him, my feet carrying me toward the kitchen. Sitting primly on a kitchen barstool, my eyes track his entrance, all pale skin and scars on display. He doesn't speak, tilting his head inquiringly.

"Pour me a glass of wine." My lips don't hesitate to utter the command, and he quickly spurs into motion, gesturing at the cabinets to his right.

"Where are they?" he asks, need barely suppressing his gravel voice. I point, then lean back on my elbows, watching him work. He's quick, pulling a random bottle and glass free and placing them on the counter. I'm mildly surprised he doesn't ask for my preference, but the label assures me it's a wine I'll enjoy.

He turns to me, lips stretched into a wide smile, placing the red liquid glistening in a crystal glass next to me.

Without acknowledging the completion of his task, my hands grip the hem of my shirt, pulling the material up and over my head, repeating the motion until I'm sitting on the stool in my bra and pants. Cool glass kisses my fingers as I wrap them around the stem of the wine glass.

Blue pupils expand, pink tongue flicking out to lick dry lips. His eyes hold a question I don't answer, taking a sip from the glass. Buried deep within me is the enjoyment of his childlike curiosity and eagerness to please. I've noted his tense posture and fidgeting fingers. Tonight, I plan to reassure him I'm his

25
A GOOD BOY

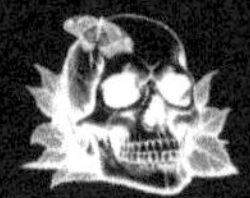

ZAIDEN

She's everything. My vision narrows to just Sarah, blocking everything else out. Her back arches, dark hair brushing the kitchen table. I don't need further instruction, hooking my fingers in the waistband of her pants. Her hips raise, aiding the slide of her scrub bottoms down her legs.

My fingers release the soft material, eyes narrowing on her lace-covered sex. Saliva collects in my mouth for a taste, but I wait for my Sarah like a good boy. Her hips wiggle slightly in invitation, a red liquid-filled glass rising to her lips.

While her throat swallows, downing the cherry-colored liquid, I dive forward, jerking her panties out of the way. I groan when her taste bursts on my tongue, blood rushing to my cock. But Sarah is in charge, commandeering my body. Her moans encourage me, a hand drifting to my hair, pressing my face firmly into her wet haven.

I lose myself in her flavor, greedily swiping my tongue into every corner of her sweet pussy, wetness staining my chin. My tongue works furiously, flicking back and forth across her swollen clit in rapid movements. My fingers glide in and out of her wet hole, moans teasing my ears, sliding down my spine. Sarah is all mine, her pleasure held in my hands.

Her legs press tightly against my head, nearly blocking out her rising moans. My mouth doesn't quit working until a loud moan shatters the illusion of quiet, ripping free from her throat. Her thighs threaten to crush my skull. My tongue keeps sampling her flavor, riding out the after-shocks that bring her hips up and down against my face.

When she goes limp, I pull back, removing my mouth from the best dessert to ever land on my tongue. Nothing can compare to her flavor or the hold she wields over me. My body eagerly awaits her next instruction, listening to the sharp exhales leaving her body.

Dazed, green eyes land on me, a soft smile fixed to her lips. She sits up, hair swinging forward, partially shielding her breasts. A jerk of her head points toward the stool next to her. Obediently, I slide onto the chair, eyes tracking her lithe body moving from her stool to straddle me.

Fingers glide through my short hair, her breath coasting across my face. Our faces are inches apart, sharing the same oxygen until her hands wrap around my cock, holding it steady as she slowly lowers herself onto it. My head falls back, eyes closing.

My nails dig into her hips. Pleasure zips down my spine, balls tightening. She feels too good, hips rocking forward as she adjusts to me.

"Dayton," she moans, snapping my eyes open to lock gazes with my raven. A pretty, red flush crawls across her skin.

"My raven," I croak, pushing and pulling her hips back and forth to help her find her pleasure. If she starts riding me, I won't be able to hold back for her. Her face eliminates the space between us, ripping a groan from me when she raises her hips and slams back down onto my waiting cock.

She's going to wreck me. It's written all in her eyes, a challenging glint hardening into emerald chips.

"Sarah," I plead, shaking my head as she does it again and again. Tremors snake their way into my legs, balls drawing up tight.

Her lips graze my ear. "Be a good boy and come for me, Dayton."

Fuck!

"Sarah!" I shout, her name leaving my lips as pleasure slams into me, shoving me off the edge with my cock still plunging in and out of Sarah's pussy.

She keeps riding me hard, never stopping while my cock jerks within her, filling her up. My hand grips her nape, pulling her face down, our mouths meeting. My tongue sweeps in, plundering what's mine. Her moans get trapped between us, mingling with my groan when I feel her walls contracting around my cock, undulating in a wave.

She keeps gliding up and down my softening cock, wringing every drop from me before slumping against my chest, face pressed into my neck. A warm feeling burns my insides. My arms tighten around the treasure lying within them.

I'm home. My little raven scraped out my innards, replacing them with her, nestling into my heart.

A fan spins lazily above me, drawing my eyes repeatedly. Sarah's head rests on my chest, fingers tracing circles on my skin. Her silky hair curls around my fingers as I twirl them, hypnotized by her and the low droning of the fan.

A sigh leaves her and my eyes close, fear rippling beneath my skin. The night was going so beautifully after we made a mess of each other downstairs. I shared my first bath with Sarah shortly after, hair still damp and resting on a pillow. The intimacy in bathing with her poured gasoline on the low burning sensation in my chest.

I think I have a name for it, but her sigh sends dread flooding my veins, tensing beneath her.

"Do I want to know everything you've done?" she asks in a soft voice.

"No," I whisper, silently begging her to not pry. Her cheek rubs back and forth across my chest. I wait, muscles refusing to relax.

"Where did you go after you burned the house?" I blink at the question, wondering where the line of questions leads.

"To Dr. Shaw's. He's letting me stay with—" Her head jerks up, wide eyes clashing with mine.

"Wait. Benji Shaw?" she asks, excitement leaping into her eyes at my nod.

"*The* Dr. Shaw? A damn pioneer in the psychology department? I'm pretty sure the hospital has a plaque with his name on it." A chuckle rumbles from my chest, shaking Sarah.

"He's just a man, my Sarah," I remind her, smiling down into her slack-jawed expression. I didn't know Dr. Shaw had such a high reputation. It makes sense.

Only he dared to look beyond what everyone saw, poking and prodding into my psyche, unearthing my motivations as a key toward recovery. His techniques regarding thought redirection helped lessen the murmur of voices in my head. He's taught me to question my delusions instead of merely accepting them as fact.

"He's a great man," I amend. Sarah wouldn't be lying in my arms, gazing at me with a tender expression, if I never crossed paths with Benji.

"You're so adorable," she says, laughing. I trail a finger across her lips.

"I think I'm in love with you," I admit, giving voice to the feeling singeing my insides.

26

CLAIMING SARAH

SARAH

My eyes widen at Dayton's confession. I didn't think it was possible to top the admission that he knew Dr. Shaw! Perhaps I take too long to reply because Dayton's expression shuts down.

I lean forward to brush my lips across his.

"You don't feel the same," he murmurs. It's not a question. And he's not wrong. Pulling back, I stare into his eyes, letting the color mesmerize me as they did the first time I looked into them in the darkened hallway of a bar.

"I need a little more time than you to get there." My fingers caress his cheek, hoping to lighten the rejection embedded in my words. Acting as shutters, his lids close, blocking his eyes from view.

"Do you think you could? Love me?" My heart squeezes painfully. If I were being honest with myself, I'm halfway there. But anger races through me at all the people who put the doubt in his mind, making him question even the possibility of someone loving him.

"Absolutely, Dayton." My lips touch his again, a ghost

of a kiss. "But promise me something?" Slowly, like the sun rising in the morning, his lids lift. My fingers brush damp strands off his forehead. Vulnerability lurks in his eyes.

"No more killings. No more kidnappings—" My back hits the mattress, Dayton rolling us before I can finish uttering my ground rules. His lips claim mine, making a promise without words. Wrapping my legs around his waist, I pull him closer, eliminating any gaps between our bodies.

His cock jerks against my slit before sliding up with the movement of his hips. Without breaking our kiss, Dayton's hand spreads my thighs wider, hips aiming his cock for my opening. I moan into his mouth, whimpering as he slowly eases himself inside of me.

"Dayton!" I gasp, pulling my mouth free.

"Mine, Sarah. Say it, and I'll promise you the fucking world. I just need to hear you say it. If you say it's possible, I will earn your love." His hips retreat before driving forward, sheathing himself fully inside of me. My pussy clenches around him, still tender from riding him earlier. Sliding my hands into his hair, I rake my nails along his scalp, enjoying the shudder that runs through him, traveling through our connected bodies.

"I'm yours, Zaiden." A whimper slips from his lips, and I give him an evil grin, deliberately using his first name. He likes it. My other hand grabs one of his ass cheeks, using it to grind his pelvis into me, stimulating my clit.

"Fuck me, Zaiden. Claim me. Prove to me that you're mine as well." Pulling his head down, I skate my lips over his ear.

"Be my good boy." He snarls, pulling his cock free and thrusting forward, slamming into me.

"Mine," he growls, yanking my hands above my head and pinning me in place. Wild eyes pierce me. He stares into my soul, cock driving in and out of me, our flesh slapping together.

"All mine. My Sarah," he mumbles, never slowing down. Pleasure coils tight within me, walls fluttering around the cock plunging deeper on each thrust. Dayton fucks me like a man possessed, never breaking my stare. When he angles his cock to target a spot deep within me, my eyes roll, moans spilling from my lips.

"Dayton," I whimper, edging closer toward euphoria, tightening my legs around his waist.

"Come for me, my raven," he croons, trailing his nose along my cheek, slowing down his rhythm. In a matter of seconds, the atmosphere shifts, transforming from wild, feral energy to tender, gentle strokes. I come apart at the seams, head thrown back, Dayton's name wheezing out of my mouth.

Lips rain kisses down my neck. Fingernails dig into my thigh. Dayton's body quivers above me like a bowstring stretched taut, his release imminent. I want it. I want it all, every broken, jagged piece of him. He calls me his raven. To me, he's a phoenix, perishing in the flames of his past, rising from the ashes brand new, altered. *Mine.*

My teeth nip his lips, tugging gently, capturing the groan he makes as he explodes inside of me. Grunts leave his mouth, hips rocking back and forth, emptying everything inside of me. My tongue swipes along his neck, collecting his taste, body going lax beneath him.

The raven and the phoenix. Together, intricately entwined, the future doesn't seem so bleak.

The End.

EPILOGUE

ZAIDEN

My hands drag down my jeans, nails clawing up on the return. Sarah sits in the driver's seat of her car, silently letting me process things. Sunlight makes the imposing house we're parked in front of sparkle, white columns standing sentry near the door. Double French doors glare at me, whispering I do not belong.

I jump when a hand lands on my leg, looking over at my raven, who smiles softly at me.

"It's okay to be nervous, Dayton, but unless you're Zoe, Zaine won't bite. Come on, let's go in and meet your brother." Air saws in and out of my open mouth. Sarah's right. I know she is.

"What if he doesn't believe me?" I ask, bringing a hand to rub at the shaved sides of my head. I didn't miss the appreciative gleam in Sarah's eyes the first time she saw my new haircut. So, every two weeks, I go to get it shaved back down when it grows out, keeping the hairstyle for her, even though I miss the way my hair would brush my jaw, hiding my scars in public.

She leans over to brush a kiss across my lips, distracting me from the what-ifs swirling in my head.

"He won't call you a liar. But we can always get a DNA test if he demands one. We can't put this off forever." Her breath brushes my lips, smelling of vanilla and strawberries from the latte and French toast we had at one of her favorite breakfast spots.

I've put this encounter off for two months, attending therapy once a week with a colleague of Sarah's, alternating medications until I discover something that doesn't make me feel like a zombie, and prepping for a surprise proposal to Sarah.

She'd let me take my time until this week, bringing it up in every conversation until I caved. My eyes shoot to her stomach, hidden behind her sundress.

She's hiding something, a voice whispers in my head, but I'm not sure if it's paranoia talking or intuition.

"Let's go," I agree, pulling back and pushing the door open, hot air ruffling my clothes. Rounding the car, Sarah entwines our hands when she reaches me, and we walk hand in hand toward the door.

ZAINE

Three weeks. Three fucking weeks is how long I held out. I snapped, craving Zoe's flavor on my tongue like a damned addict. My mouse gives me a coy smile, pulling the straps of her dress down, exposing her full breasts and nipples a shade darker than her skin. Saliva pools in my mouth, and I pray to all that is unholy that Zaria stays down for her nap.

The bed dips as I crawl to my pet, my cock an excruciating ache in my pelvis, but I can't put it inside her for another three fucking weeks. That wait is agonizing, and I'm seriously reconsidering filling her up with another child. I can't take not having her writhing beneath me, moans in my ear, walls clenching around my cock.

My hand brushes her bare thigh, sliding up and shoving the material of her nightgown out of the way. A lacy red thong shields her sex from me, and I can't wait to shove it aside to have Zoe's nectar coating my tongue. Blood rushes in my ears and—

Knock. Knock.

"Son of a bitch!" I shout, momentarily forgetting my sleeping daughter in her bassinet, who wakes with a startled cry. Zoe slaps my hand away with a disapproving glare, reaching down into the attached bassinet for Zaria.

Can a man not eat pussy in peace? For fuck's sake!

"Yes, Tessa," I snap, patience disappearing like smoke. My eyes never leave the breast Zoe brings to Zaria's grasping mouth, a frustrated cry leaving her when she can't latch. If I wasn't so damn starved, I'd find the fussy infant amusing in her desperate grab for my fiancé's nipple.

"You have company downstairs, sir," Tessa speaks through the door, wise enough not to enter. I'm liable to commit fucking murder for thirty uninterrupted minutes alone with my future bride.

Whoever is downstairs better fucking pray I don't follow through with it, getting out of bed with an aching cock straining my slacks.

SARAH

The housekeeper—Tess, I believe, is her name—answered the door and led us into an opulent sitting room. Red drapes and slate faux wood blinds shield the sun's rays from infiltrating the spacious room. Three chaise lounges encircle a glass coffee table. A full-service bar rests along one wall, and built-in bookshelves boasting a variety of titles line the other wall.

Dayton paces the length of the room, hand rubbing at his nape, boots sliding across the plush carpet. If he notices the decor, he doesn't comment, eyes bouncing in every direction. He's restless, and I don't know the words to calm him. He'd made so much progress in the two months since he showed up at my job hours before I helped deliver Ms. Cynthia's child.

Sliding a hand down the front of my dress, I contemplate how to deliver the news of our own child. The words always get stuck on my tongue. Only Dr. Leblanc knows. Three failed IVFs in the twenty-plus years since I adopted Lauren, and my miracle child comes from the seed of a Lasher. I am not oblivious to the irony.

"You're going to burn a hole in my floor," a smooth voice clips from the open doorway. Both of our heads snap toward Zaine, cool blue eyes jumping from me and back to Dayton, who rubs his hands up and down his pants legs.

"Zaine. How's mother and child?" I ask, breaking the ice with small talk. His lips don't shift into a smile, but a glimmer of appreciation slips into his eyes.

"They're well. We're about three weeks out from Zoe's checkup to make sure everything healed up nicely. Thank you again for helping to deliver my daughter." Sincere gratitude enters his voice, and I bite back my smile, knowing full well why he's keeping track of Zoe's six-week appointment.

"Of course, you're welcome. Anytime something is wrong, don't be afraid to call." My eyes dart to Dayton, who hasn't uttered a word, standing still as a statue across the room.

"Dayton," I coax, jerking my head at Zaine meaningfully. He jerks forward, still not speaking, and Zaine's eyebrows shoot up, slanting a questioning look my way. I shrug, gesturing with my hand for Dayton to take the lead.

ZAIDEN

A blond, blue-eyed devil stares me down, lips set in a firm line. What the hell do I say to him? Your dad railed my mom?

His arms cross over his chest, and he cocks a brow, impatience written across his frame.

"My name is Zaiden. Zaiden Dayton Daniels," I start, palms brushing my jeans. Smooth features ripple in a flinch.

"Interesting name," he remarks, a strange intensity entering his eyes.

"Thanks. My mom named me after my brother. He died when he was a babe." I let the words hang in the air, wariness, and pain flickering across my big brother's face.

"Zachary Lasher is my father." My eyes shift to Sarah. Giving me a wan smile, she saunters over, lacing our fingers. Leeching her strength, I finish the sordid tale. "My mom was Morgan Daniels. They met at a grief group, and, I guess, one thing led to another."

"He cheated on my mom," Zaine mutters, looking away from me. I say nothing, letting him process my confession, waiting for the inevitable rejection. To add fuel to the fire, I supply, "I have schizophrenia." Sarah elbows me, glaring up at me. I shrug, mentally prepared for Zaine to throw us out.

"You're my brother," he whispers, eyes finding their way back to me. Through a dry mouth, I reply, "Yes." One word. One word that spurs him into motion.

Zaine rushes at me and I rip my hand from Sarah, stepping in front of her and getting caught in a bear hug. He yanks me into his chest, arms banding around me. Air wheezes out of my lungs. I only allowed my mother and Sarah to get this close, stunned stiff.

A hand pats my back with rough slaps, and I hear Zaine whispering, "My brother," over and over. Fuck! A dam breaks, and I return the hug, face crumbling and emotions leaking free. He hugs me through it, rocking us side to side.

I found them, Mom. I found my brothers.

AFTERWORD

Thank you for reading *Claiming Sarah*.
Turn the page for a peek at Daddy Dayton.
And stay tuned for details about "Dalton".

ACKNOWLEDGMENTS

I'd love to keep this short and sweet as this book is releasing a week after Escaping Xavier.

I want to thank Aliyah Golden for the edit and Stacey for the proofread. I appreciate both of you helping me polish up Zaiden and Sarah's story.

Speaking of polishing up, thank you Alpha/Beta team: Elise, Jordyn, Stacey, and Tanya. Special thanks to Dasha for the constructive criticism that lead to me expanding this story from my first draft.

Thank you Clare for managing the street/ARC team. More thanks to the street and ARC team for supporting me. And another thanks to Elise for everything she does for me, day in and day out. She's truly my number one fan.

If I missed anyone, I'm sorry. I truly appreciate all the help I've received on my author journey.

Thank you reader for picking up my book and giving this newbie a chance.

Best wishes,
    Mae

ABOUT THE AUTHOR

Mae K. Knight is an emerging author of dark and taboo romances.

She lives in Louisiana and can be found studying for her nursing degree or powerlifting when she's not dreaming up stories. She believes she has a morbid sense of humor and tries to incorporate this into her writing

Her books will take you on a wild ride you never asked to embark on. Buckle up. If you like your twisted romances with a dash of taboo, you've arrived at the right place. Enter Knight's den of inequity. Only the depraved enter and the brave leave...

* 9 7 9 8 3 3 0 4 6 3 0 9 1 *